I0625158

A COMPANY OF BONES

A TENNY MATEO MYSTERY

BOOK TWO

E.B. WHEELER

Rowan Ridge
Press

A Company of Bones: A Tenny Mateo Mystery

Copyright © 2023 by E.B. Wheeler

All rights reserved. No part of this book may be reproduced in any form or by any means without permission in writing from the publisher.

This book is a work of fiction. Names, characters, places, and events in this book are either the products of the author's imagination or are used fictitiously.

ISBN 978-1-960033-03-1

First Printing February 2023

Published by Rowan Ridge Press, Utah, USA

Cover design © Rowan Ridge Press

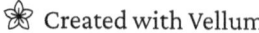 Created with Vellum

For my grandparents,
with many thanks for your stories

CHAPTER ONE

I was going to lose my brother, Javier, in the Utah desert. I steadied my Vest Pocket Kodak with one hand and used the other to free my skirt from the saber-pointed leaves of a yucca. I was no slackster when it came to hiking, but Javi bounded ahead of me like a jackrabbit, skipping around red rocks and sagebrush. Not watching for rattlesnakes basking under the oppressive sun.

"Javi!" I called. "Be careful of—"

He vanished. One minute, I could see his lanky, teenaged form and dark hair among some shrubby junipers, then it was like the desert had swallowed him.

I jolted to a stop and put my hand on my stomach. Images came back to me of when we were young in the Mormon Colonies in Mexico and the revolutionaries had come. Hiding among the thick brush by the river. Trying to keep him quiet and safe. Afraid our family would be torn apart, and we'd never see each other again.

"Javi!"

The heat and the stillness smothered my call. I hurried to where he had disappeared. The red sand shooshed beneath my boots and a jackrabbit burst from the sage and dashed away, but no other sound answered me. We were too far from the road to hear the occasional car or wagon, the cattle were farther afield, and there was no water nearby. Just the wide blue sky and the sweltering silence of the red rocks.

"Javi?"

"I'm here, Tenny!" came his muffled voice.

A narrow crevice ran along the ground between the junipers. Javi popped his head out of the opening and grinned.

Relief flooded through me, leaving me shaky. "That's not funny!" I said. "We shouldn't get separated!"

"You worry too much."

"It's dangerous out here."

He rolled his eyes. "'I'm watching out for scorpions, and this isn't the first time I've explored this place."

I knelt down by the crevice and glanced over my shoulder. "Bo Young runs his cattle out here."

"I'm pretty sure he doesn't run with them, and we're not going to bother his cows. Wait til you see what I found last week. When you take pictures of it, we'll be famous!"

"Down in that cave?" I asked, peering past him into the dimness. My mouth went dry just thinking about the tight, dark space.

"It's not a cave. You *have* to see."

I swallowed hard and double-checked that my camera was secure on its strap. Just lowering my feet into the narrow space, my chest tightened, and my breath came in short gasps for fear of the air running short. A wave of dizziness washed over me at the dank smell of cool rocks and dirt. I wasn't as slim as my little brother, so I wriggled to squeeze through the opening, sending a shower of sand ahead of me.

The crevice reached about six feet down. The red sandstone walls crowded us, and deep, chilly sand swallowed my boots. Even with the sun hot overhead, the air here was cool. I paused to catch my breath, to convince my lungs I wasn't suffocating. I fixed my gaze on the narrow strip of blue sky overhead, then noticed the walls. They'd been worn smooth, shaped into unexpected curves, faintly marked by ripples. Like—

"Water," I said. "When storms come, the water washes through here and scours the walls."

"Isn't it great?" Javi asked.

"It's beautiful."

Though, I was grateful for the cloudless skies. The thought of being trapped in there when the waters roared through made my stomach clench. Still, this was worthy of using some of my precious film.

I turned the camera's slim, metal body over in my hands and pulled out the front plate holding the lens until the bellows were fully open. In this dim light, I would need a long exposure time. I focused on the ripples in the wall about six feet in front of me. It would be stunning in color, like the photos *National Geographic* had experimented with using a special process involving potato starch—though the time and expense to develop such images was beyond me. Even in black and white, the light and shadows would make an interesting photo.

I snapped a couple of angles, bracing my elbow on the wall to keep the images steady. After each one, I opened the little slot on the back of the camera and used the metal stylus to make a note of the date and place of the photo so the information would be preserved on the side of each negative.

A little shower of sand cascaded over the edge of the narrow wash. I brushed off my sleeve and studied the soft sand on the floor, trickled in from above by wind and passing animals and sculpted by past floods. It changed slowly, but it was never the same. The moment I captured on film could be gone in an hour.

Click.

It was mine now, safe from the changes tomorrow would bring. I pushed the lens back in. Without the distraction of the camera, the walls felt too close again, making it hard to breathe.

"We should start for home," I said.

Javi laughed. "You haven't even seen the best part."

He squeezed ahead of me and picked his way through the deep sand and around the undulations of the walls, which grew narrower and higher as he went. My throat tightened, and I squeezed my eyes shut. I wasn't going to leave my brother. With hands on both walls, as though I could prevent the grainy sandstone from closing tighter and crushing me, I followed him down the narrow wash. I hoped he really had found something amazing.

I made a little extra money writing advice letters for the Kane County newspaper as "Dear Grace," but our homestead was struggling ever since the war when prices for everything dropped. We could use more money—and interesting articles and pictures might provide it. The camera on its strap bounced against my chest, and sweat trickled down my back despite the cool air.

"When are you going to tell me about this place?" I asked, shaking my foot to rearrange the sand that had slithered into my boot.

"I'm not. You just have to see it."

I rolled my eyes. Much to my relief, the wash widened until I no longer scraped against the walls while climbing over or around boulders not yet worn away by flash floods. We ducked under a log as thick as Javi's waist that some past storm had wedged with brutal finality against the walls.

The light grew brighter, and our narrow little wash opened into a dry stream bed. I took a deep breath of sagebrush-scented air as we stepped into the warm sunlight and Javi guided us through the wider canyon. The cliffs still rose above us, but here our path was open and clear. The sand slipped under our feet, and the quiet hung heavy around us. I kept one hand on my camera, wondering what Javi had discovered out here. The desert could be surprising, dull and brown one moment, and the next revealing some hidden wonder. I wished my camera could capture the desert the way my mother captured the layers of colored sand in little jars, but at least I could snap pictures of the dramatic scenery.

"Here," Javi said, pointing to a series of indentations that looked like steps going up the side of the cliff. He puffed out his chest and grinned.

"Uh." I didn't want to let him know how disappointing the cliff wall was. "Those are very interesting." But not interesting enough to make a news story. Barely interesting enough to spend any film on.

He laughed. "Not the steps. What's at the top."

I'd rather climb up than squeeze down another narrow canyon. I double-checked my camera strap so I could keep my hands free. The steps carved into the cliff face were narrow and uneven, and I questioned if they were manmade or natural. But Javi must have used them before. He scrambled ahead of me with confidence.

I braced my hands on the sandy-feeling stones. The steps were steep and didn't cut far into the cliff face, but my feet and fingers found easy purchase. Only somewhat hampered by my skirts, I climbed, expecting to reach the top of the canyon.

The steps didn't reach the top, though. They ended at a ledge. On the ledge was a round stone hut built into the cliffside—the sort abandoned hundreds of years before.

"Wow!" I said.

The desert whisked the word away and answered with a deep silence—a reminder that I was no more significant to the red rocks than a jackrabbit or a coyote. Even the junipers in the canyon had seen other generations of humans come and go and would last far longer than I.

I knelt beside Javi to peer through the low door. Inside the house were several pieces of pottery with black and tan geometric patterns. One of them still held dried-up cobs of corn. Doughnut-shaped turquoise beads lay scattered on the floor as if they had been snapped off someone's neck.

Something that looked like a corn cob doll also lay to one side of the room. My heart twinged, and I longed to reach out and touch the little toy that had been loved and abandoned so long ago. But I didn't cross the threshold.

There were a few other cliff houses like this scattered here and there around Kanab. Nothing big like the ones we had heard about in Colorado and New Mexico—palaces in the cliffs—but there was still something special about being a place that had been undisturbed for so long.

"I wonder why they left," Javi said.

"I don't know. Maybe some kind of danger. Enemies. A flood—or a drought."

Water was a tricky thing in the desert: too often scarce, and then when it did come, it roared down the gullies with terrible fury.

"Do you think we should go in?" Javi asked. "I was afraid to when I first found it."

I shook my head. "No, we should leave it alone."

"Abuela would say there are ghosts." Javi chuckled nervously.

"I'm not sure she'd be wrong. It feels kind of sacred. Like it doesn't want to be disturbed. It's a... a memorial to the dead." My mother's Scotch and Mormon beliefs were vague on the role of ghosts, but on Papa's side of the family, Abuela was Catholic and Spanish, and she would say that the spirits of the dead were jealous of the objects that connected them to this world.

Javi cast a longing look into the cliff house. "I bet those beads and things are worth a lot of money."

I stared at the turquoise scattered on the floor. He was

right. Some people paid good money for old Indian artifacts. And we needed the money. Some locals had no problem collecting or selling the treasures they found out in the desert.

I sighed and shook my head. "I don't think it's ours to take."

Javi frowned, then his face brightened again. "But you can take pictures, can't you?"

"Oh! Of course." There seemed no harm in that. I snapped several photos, especially focused on the beads and the intriguing doll, and etched little notes about each for later.

I backed away from the entrance and stood to peer at the steep steps. "Now, we have to manage to get down without breaking our necks."

Javi laughed. "No you don't. There are hand and footholds that go to the top, too."

"We could have just come straight here?" I asked, exasperated as I remembered the crushing walls of the little side canyon.

"It's tricky to climb down, and it's not as fun."

I reminded myself that I did not want to strangle my little brother.

We climbed up without much trouble, though we were both dirty and sweaty by the time we pulled ourselves onto the top of the rim. I just wanted to lie in the shade of the juniper trees for a moment.

The quiet pressed on my ears, the only sound our ragged breaths. Then, a low buzz set my teeth on edge. It quickly grew louder. A plane. Memories of the Great War washed over me, but I pushed them away. I might always hate tight spaces after trying to aid dying men in the tunnels and trenches of the Western Front, but I had developed different feelings about the approach of a plane. Thrilling, unwanted feelings. Planes were rare in Kane County, Utah, but Victor Holbrook sometimes flew this way. Every time he did, he left me riled up and confused with his teasing. His attentions were enough that Mother and Abuela gave me significant looks whenever he came our way, but I didn't know if he was trying to court me or torment me.

I tilted my head to see if the plane would pass over, and if it was actually Victor. After a few moments, I could make out his Jenny biplane with the number 976 on the sides. My heart leaped, though I chided it to be still—to be cautious.

Victor was flying low. Maybe he had stopped to see my family and was looking for Javi and me. As low as he was flying, we would be able to see each other clearly. I stood and stepped out from the juniper trees to wave.

He tipped his wing in acknowledgment. That let me see that he wasn't alone in the plane. His passenger was female, blonde, and likely young and pretty. He was probably not looking for us, then. My cheeks burned at my foolishness, and my throat felt like I had swallowed sand. The buzz of the engine faded as he flew on, leaving Javi and me alone in the desert.

CHAPTER TWO

By the time Javi and I hiked back home, the sun had dipped low, and the western sky glowed orange like a distant fire on the horizon. The cool evening breeze brought me the clean scent of the laundry we'd hung to dry that morning. I'd have to bring it in that night before going to sleep, but it was worth it to have an afternoon of freedom.

Javi chattered on about the narrow wash and the cliff house, but I had sunk into my thoughts. Not about Victor—I wouldn't let myself brood over him—but about the pictures. If they were good, and if I published them, what would happen to that little stone house that stood as a memorial to the past? If I published a story about it in the local paper, people would probably figure out where it was. Some of them would respect its secrets, but not everyone.

What if I sent the photos and a story to a magazine like *National Geographic*? I didn't know what they paid, but it would establish my name as a journalist, and I could be vague about the location. But the pictures would have to be really good. I clutched my camera. I didn't want to waste any film, but I needed to finish this roll so I could have it developed.

"Or we could charge people for tours. What do you think, Tenny?" Javi asked.

I blinked away my dreams of literary fame and tried to remember what Javi was talking about. "Tours of the cliff house? No, people would disturb it, and then there would be nothing left to show anyone."

He huffed. "What about just the wash?"

I wanted to say that he shouldn't get anyone close to the cliff house, but we weren't the only locals who hiked around the desert. Maybe taking people there on tours would let him control what they saw. I didn't think many locals would pay for that, but I didn't want to crush all of his ideas. "Why not? As long as you don't go when it's raining."

"Like it ever rains around here. Hey, look! It's Victor!"

Victor's biplane sat in our cow pasture, its bovine neighbors keeping a wary distance. My stomach clenched. Had Victor brought his lady friend to meet my family?

Victor jogged up to meet us, a wide, silly grin on his face. "Hey, Javi. Hey, Doll. I'm glad to see you made it home all right. Your mom was worried. She's worked up a scolding for you, Javi. You'd better get inside before she thinks of more to add to it."

Javi rolled his eyes and stomped off ahead of us.

Victor turned his attention back to me. He took my hand —the one that held the Kodak—and pulled me closer so he could study the camera. The warmth of his fingers against mine was dangerously distracting.

"Nice," he said, meeting my eyes. "You get any good pictures out there?"

Part of me wanted to tell him all about the stone house, but then I remembered the pretty blonde, so I just shrugged. "I won't know until I develop them."

"Well, I have exciting news—a surprise—and it will give you even more to take pictures of."

My chest tightened as I thought again of his passenger, and I couldn't meet his eyes. "What, a wedding?"

"Not quite yet, but maybe soon," he said, his voice low.

I pulled my hand away, refusing to look at him. I didn't want him to see that I was hurt. He'd always been a flirt, but it had only been a matter of time before some pretty girl pinned him down. He was probably taking her north to meet his family, and we were a convenient stopping point. "You needn't have taken time away from your guest to come see us."

He was silent for a moment, then burst out laughing. "Don't tell me you're jealous, Sweetheart?"

"I'm not your sweetheart."

I walked toward the house, forcing him to march a quick pace to keep up.

"Don't fret, Miss Hortencia Mateo." He tried—and failed —to say it with a proper Spanish accent. "I brought a whole troupe of guests here with me, but I wouldn't be rude enough to drop them on your family without an invitation."

I gave him a speculative look. He could only fit one passenger in his plane. What was he up to?

My mother put her head out the door, her red hair glowing in the light from the oil lamps inside. She smiled warmly at Victor. "Are you staying, then, Mr. Holbrook?"

Our dog Daisy darted out the door and bounded to Victor, tail waving furiously.

He scratched her favorite spot behind her ears. "I'd love to have dinner, Ma'am, but I'll be bunking down closer to town on this visit."

I frowned, puzzling that over, and dusted off my boots on the mat by the kitchen door.

"Don't you want to know why I'm staying in town?" Victor asked, watching me with a teasing smile.

"I'm sure it's none of my business. You're a grown man and can do as you please."

"I wish that were the case! Come on, I want to tell your whole family my news."

I followed him inside, curious and a little sick. The spicy scent of Abuela's paella washed over me, making my mouth water at the thought of the rice, chicken, and vegetables simmering in tomato sauce. Abuela, standing at the wood-burning stove, gave us a look warning us not to get in the way of her cooking, and we hurried past her to the dining room. Mother was setting the table, and I could see Papa in the living room picking out a song on his salterio, and my sister Rosie and Mel Young with their heads together over the crystal radio set.

Victor grabbed the stack of napkins before I could and followed Mother, setting one beside each plate.

"So, what brings you to Kanab this time?" Mother asked Victor. "Some secret mission, you hinted?"

She glanced my direction, and I blushed.

He grinned. "Well, it won't be a secret for long, so here it is: I'm here with a crew from Hollywood. They're filming a Western movie right here in Kane County."

So, his blonde passenger was a Hollywood starlet? At least he hadn't mentioned her in specific—nothing about a fiancée.

Mother straightened, her expression calculating. "All those Hollywood people coming to town?"

"Yep," Victor said. "They're all going to need food and places to stay, and there will be lots of jobs for the locals."

Javi poked his head in the dining room. "Did you say they're making a movie here, and we can be in it?"

"You'll have to audition," Victor warned him, "but even if you don't get a part, they need people to build sets, cook meals, take care of the horses."

"All those jobs!" Papa said, coming up behind Javi. "That's just what Kanab needs."

"And you brought them here?" Mother asked Victor.

"That depends," Victor said, glancing at me. "Do you like the idea or not?"

Papa laughed. "Of course we like it."

Rosie and Mel came up behind him. Mel adjusted the tin mask that hid his war injuries. They probably wouldn't put him on screen, but he would appreciate a way to earn some money behind the scenes and get out from under his father Bo's controlling thumb. Mel would probably take Rosie away with him when he'd saved up enough to escape and start over somewhere else. I was happy for Rosie, but the thought of her leaving made my chest ache.

Victor gave Mel a nod of recognition. There was a bond between us—we'd all been Over There. The war had left its mark on each of us in different ways. Ways that weren't always obvious to everyone else, who were doing their best to forget the war and the influenza, but those of us who had been there would never forget.

Victor smiled at Mother. "I encouraged the idea, but it was the Parry Brothers that pitched it to the Hollywood folks. They've been talking up southern Utah to everyone who will listen, and they found the right audience with these fellows wanting to film a proper Western."

"Some sort of cowboys and Indians story?" I asked.

Victor grinned. "Nope. The tale of Zorro, the Spanish Robin Hood of Old Mexico."

"Zorro!" Javi cried, lisping the Z with a proper Castilian accent learned from Abuela. "That's perfect! We'll get roles for sure. I'll bring my guitar, too. Maybe I can become a famous actor."

"Ha!" Mother said. "First you'll be famous for having the dirtiest hands at the dinner table. Go wash up!"

I watched him dash into the kitchen, worrying my lip. "I'm glad there will be jobs, but are the people from Hollywood safe? I've heard stories..."

"Believe them!" Victor said. "You'll have to watch your back around them—especially the actors. But that's more about vying for roles and influence. They're not going to lure your teenaged brother into a life of alcohol and depravity."

Mother went pale at that. "I would hope not!"

Victor didn't sound too admiring of the Hollywood crowd. Did that include his starlet?

"What is taking so long?" Abuela called from the kitchen. "The paella is going to burn!"

Papa grinned. "The burnt rice at the bottom is my favorite, Mama."

"*Qué malo!*" Abuela grumbled.

Javi hurried back into the dining room, his hands still damp from washing. He glanced between our parents. "You're going to let us audition, aren't you?"

Mother exchanged a look with Papa.

"It's worth trying for the extra income," Papa said. "There's not as much to do around the homestead right now."

We'd planted the cool-weather crops, and it was too early for the ones that liked warm nights. We needed the money, but did we really need Hollywood?

Mother sighed. "All right. But I want you all to stay together, be careful, don't let anything turn your head."

"When do we need to go?" I asked Victor.

"They're starting things up tomorrow—not wasting any time."

"Well," Papa said. "You'd all better eat a good meal, then. You'll need your energy tomorrow."

We devoured the paella, much to Abuela's satisfaction.

"You are too skinny," she said, shaking a finger at Victor. "And you!" She poked at Mel, who grinned sheepishly. "I also made raisin cake. Everyone must eat some. *Comed!*"

No one complained about the cake, and the conversation was cheerful. I couldn't get my mind off *National Geographic* and Hollywood. It felt like everything we tried to keep the homestead alive eroded away the refuge it provided us—

bringing in outsiders, splitting the family. Couldn't we just stay safe and cozy together, and the rest of the world could leave us alone? But there was fuel to buy, equipment to repair, little luxuries and conveniences we couldn't provide for ourselves.

We all helped clean up after dinner. When I took the scraps out to feed the pigs, Victor caught up with me.

"You're really worried about Hollywood, huh?" he asked.

"I'm worried about Javier. And, yes, everyone else."

He frowned and looked off into the distance. "It's just—you know I'm not always good at saying the right thing, so I hope I don't give offense—but you went to France in the middle of a war. He's not even trying to hop across the border to Arizona."

I stared down at the bucket of scraps, broken eggshells glowing in the dim light. "You know why I went over there?"

Victor shook his head, watching me closely.

"It was the Zimmerman Telegraph—the one from Germany encouraging Mexico to invade the US."

"Sure, that got everyone fired up," Victor said.

"Yes, but my family fled from Mexico already, from the Revolution. I remember trying to keep Rosie and Javi safe, and I knew the US troops down there on the border weren't very well trained. I was afraid for my family. Afraid the war was going to come for them again. I thought if I could help in some small way, I could help the war end faster and keep it from overtaking them."

'That's a heavy burden to carry, trying to keep your whole family safe."

"It probably sounds silly."

"No, I think it's noble of you." He smiled. "Maybe a touch overly ambitious."

"Yes, well, I know we're not always safe here, either, after... after the murders." Victor knew about the bootlegger murders too well, having been accused—and cleared—of being involved. "But that just makes me more afraid." I gestured out to the homestead. "This is all we have. It's so hard to keep it going, and if we lose it, we have to start over. We've done it before, but now my parents are getting older, and if our family splits up..."

Victor nodded. "It's frightening." He reached down and put his hand next to mine on the bucket's handle. "I admire your independence, but maybe I can help, too?"

I let him take the bucket. That was an easy enough burden to relinquish. But the rest of it? What could anyone do? When I thought about the future, I felt like I was standing in a wash, trying to hold back a flash flood that would scour away everyone I loved.

CHAPTER THREE

The next morning, Javi, Rosie, and I woke extra early. Javi shambled out into chilly, predawn twilight to milk the cow, and I pulled on a shawl and hurried to feed the chickens while Rosie lit the stove for breakfast.

"What should we wear?" Rosie asked back in our bedroom, holding up the dress she wore when she and Abuela went to Mass—a long ride to a neighboring town they made only a few times a year.

"I'm not sure." Since I attended Mormon services every Sunday, my best dress was a little less crisp.

"I'm dressing as a vaquero!" Javi called from his room.

I laughed. "Maybe that's a good approach."

Rosie shrugged and put on her best dress. I decided on a simple dress with a low waist and wide collar—one I could move in and wouldn't worry about ruining. I had seen my friend Ginny's fashion catalogs. No matter how well we dressed, we wouldn't measure up to Hollywood's standards.

I put on my cloche hat and went out to crank up the Model T for the ride into town.

The rumble of Victor's plane sounded over the early morning noises of chickens and cattle. Javi, dressed in old Levis, chaps, and a Tom Mix hat with its wide brim and tall crown, ran out to watch the biplane land in the pasture. The cattle fled, lowing in protest.

Victor climbed out of the biplane—no passenger this time—and hopped down smoothly to wave at us. I couldn't help admiring his confidence as he strolled across the field, making a mock bow to the cattle who watched him from a wary distance.

Victor climbed the fence and smiled at us. "I thought I'd come back and make sure you hadn't chickened out of auditioning."

I folded my arms. "Of course not."

He winked at me. "I didn't mean you, Sweetheart. After the Western Front, I'm sure you can handle Hollywood."

"Are you spending a lot of time in Hollywood?" Javi asked him.

"Sure. I've been doing some flying in Hollywood, and they've got me out here running errands for them. I'm just waiting for them to make a war movie so I can fly in it."

"Have you been in any other movies?" Javi asked.

"I've done some stunt flying for a few of them. Haven't you spotted me in any of them?"

"We don't get to see movies very often out here," I said defensively. The nearest theaters were in Panguitch or St.

George. We didn't even have electricity or telephones. It irked me to think of Victor surrounded by beautiful, sophisticated people in California. Much more than distance separated Hollywood from Kanab or Pahreah.

"I'm going to tell Rosie to hurry up," Javi said and dashed back into the house.

With Javi gone, Victor stepped closer to me.

"You glad to see me? You always promise you'll miss me if I leave."

I smirked. "I distinctly remember only promising to see if I *would* miss you."

"Well, and did you?" His voice was low, almost husky, and he looked at me intently.

I shrugged, unable to meet his eyes. "Maybe a little. It is more interesting with you around."

He grinned broadly. "I knew you'd miss me."

"Hmph. And I suppose you've been too busy in Hollywood to miss... anything here in Utah?" Too distracted by blonde starlets, perhaps?

"No need to be jealous. I've just been doing what I promised—finding a legal way to earn money with my flying. That's what you wanted, isn't it?"

"Well, I'm glad you're not running bootlegged liquor anymore! And glad that Hollywood hasn't made you too high and mighty for us."

"Never," Victor said with a wink. "If being a flying ace didn't do it, what would?"

"Ace! Since when?"

"If you count all the movie planes I've shot down, I'm better than the Red Baron."

"Ha!"

"But here I am. And I've brought Hollywood with me."

I frowned at that.

"You're still worried?"

"It's going to fill Javi's head with ideas."

Victor laughed. "He's a teenaged boy. He'll fill his own head with ideas. At least this way, he'll get a taste of being famous without having to leave home."

"And I suppose Hollywood couldn't leave all its problems behind."

Victor looked thoughtful. "That would probably be too much to ask. They'll mostly keep to themselves, though."

"Are they going to hire many locals to work on the set?"

"Sure! Think of how much work it would be to drag people up from Hollywood just to stand around in the background. They'll also eat at local restaurants, pay for room and board. It'll be great for business."

"I hope so," I admitted. It had never been easy farming in the desert, and it only seemed to get harder.

Victor elbowed me gently. "You've got to get with the times, Doll. Do you want to fly over there with me?"

I glanced at the biplane, remembering the mix of thrill and terror in taking off and the peaceful calm of gliding above the desert canyons.

"Yes, but not today. I was going to invite Ginny to come with us to the auditions. You take Javi instead. He'd love to fly again."

"Not worried it'll give him the flying bug?"

"No, he's too full of the Hollywood bug for now."

Victor smiled and gave me directions to the canyon

where Hollywood had set up camp. Javi was more than happy to take my place in the biplane, and Rosie and I drove the Model T over to Ginny's farm.

Ginny was in her rabbit barn brushing one of her angoras. She managed to look glamorous even in overalls fluffed up with bits of angora wool and her blonde bob pinned messily back from her face. She smiled a greeting, and I paused to pet the rabbit's long, silky fur. Ginny sheared it and sold it to mills up north, who used it to make a luxuriously soft, warm yarn—her innovative way to supplement her homestead's income.

"What brings you out here?" Ginny asked.

"They're going to be filming a movie in Kanab and hiring locals as extras, set workers—things like that. Do you want to come with us to get some extra work?"

"A movie, really?" she asked. "How much are they paying?"

"More than nothing, which is what I'll get if I'm just sitting at home."

"The newspaper gig isn't paying anymore?"

Ginny was one of the only people who knew that I wrote letters as the advice columnist Miss Grace. "It is, but Barry's struggling to keep people reading. The paper may fold."

Ginny's eyes lit up, and she took my arm. "Give them another reason to read, then. People love Hollywood gossip. Miss Grace should write up some gossip to add to her advice letters."

I bit my lip. "I don't know. Gossip can be destructive."

"Oh, I don't mean nasty gossip. Just little tidbits. Who seems to like whom, who's doing especially well on their lines. It can be positive gossip but give people a peek inside the Hollywood world. It'll be good for the movie and for the paper."

I brightened. "That's a good idea."

She grinned. "Of course it is."

"But it means I have to actually get a part as an extra so I can see what's going on."

"Then we'd better get moving." She gently picked up the rabbit to return it to its cage. "No, wait. I need to change, and you..." Ginny studied me. "We need a different hat for you. Hats with little brims are in this year."

Rosie preferred to stay with the car, but I deferred to Ginny's taste and let her dress me up a little more. Unlike me, she was born for the styles that flattered boyish figures with their low waists and straight lines, but I had to admit I looked more presentable—and fashionable—when she was finished with me.

For herself, Ginny debated over an angora wool shawl, but finally settled on an angora sash to go with the sleek dress swishing around her knees. "Maybe I'll start a trend."

She might.

We walked outside, and Ginny waved down Sam Ellis, her ranch foreman.

"There's going to be a Hollywood movie filmed in Kanab," Ginny said. "We can both afford to take a little time off if you want to audition."

"And dress up as some fake Indian to get killed by a white cowboy? No thanks."

Sam was Paiute, though he'd been raised by a white Mormon family.

I spoke up. "The movie is Zorro—you know, the Spanish hero?"

"Let me know when there's an Indian hero," he said, throwing in a grin to show us—or rather Ginny, I guessed—that there were no hard feelings.

"Fair enough." Ginny smiled in return. "But let the ranch hands know they can audition as long as they get their work done around here, too."

We drove over to the canyon where the Hollywood folks were busy constructing buildings with no fronts or roofs and the fronts of building with nothing behind them. All fake, but it would look good on the silver screen. The only real buildings on the site belonged to the family who had rented out their ranch to Hollywood, and those stood in the background, maybe not picturesque enough for the movies.

It seemed like everyone in town was lined up to try out for a part or get work on the set. Well, no wonder. We all needed the extra money.

Javi ran up to greet us.

"Took you long enough! I already auditioned, and I got a part. I'm going to be a vaquero. I might even get to shoot at Zorro."

That sounded promising. Even just one family member making extra money from the movie would help us out. He skipped off and left us to wait our turn. The line moved surprisingly fast. I realized that they weren't looking for acting skills, just a certain type. The people were quickly sorted into those who would play vaqueros, ladies, Indians, drunks, and other characters Hollywood deemed necessary to recreate Old California.

When we reached the front, the casting director gave us a quick look over and glanced down at a sheet in his hands. He pointed to Rosie.

"Indian maiden."

"I'm not Indian," Rosie said.

He shrugged. "You want the part?"

"I—I suppose."

"Right, move over there, then, to get your schedule."

He glanced at me, and I could see him dismissing me. Then he saw Ginny, and he slowly rose to his feet to inspect her more closely.

She folded her arms and raised an eyebrow at him. "You like what you see?"

"You've got spunk!" he said, grinning at her. "You'll be one of our beautiful Spanish ladies!"

Ginny laughed. "Me?"

"Don't pretend to be modest, my dear. You know you're a pretty picture."

"But I'm blonde!"

"The film is black and white. It doesn't matter. That'll take care of you lot. Next!"

I stood staring stupidly at him for a moment. He had nothing for me? Not Indian maiden? Not Spanish lady? Hortencia Mateo wasn't Spanish enough for him? I wanted to give him some of Ginny's attitude, but it wouldn't do me any good. While a costumer whisked Ginny away, I slunk off in defeat.

"Miss Mateo!" Victor jogged up to me. "So, what did they give you?"

"Rejection."

"What?" The look of outrage on his face soothed my hurt feelings a little.

"They cast Rosie as an Indian maiden and Ginny as a Spanish lady. Nothing for me."

"That's ridiculous. I should have gotten you here earlier. They've probably just filled most of the roles. Hey, it's not too late to put on a poncho and sombrero and try out for a vaquero."

I laughed in spite of myself. "I'm glad for Javi and Rosie. Just, Ginny gave me an idea that I liked. I thought about writing about the gossip—the fun stuff—and maybe Barry would give me more work. It might help the paper, too. I've got a camera. I could even take pictures."

"That is a good idea. Look, there's more going on here than just sitting in front of a movie camera. You could help with costumes or make-up or food."

"I'm not a bad cook," I said.

"There you go. I'll introduce you to some people. And, it may work out better for you, because the extras aren't on set all the time, but the behind-the-scenes people are here every day."

"Thank you," I said, both embarrassed and gratified by Victor's attention.

We headed over to the food tent. Outside of it stood Bo Young, arms crossed and chatting with a stranger sweating in a suit. Bo smirked when he saw me.

"Ah, Miss Mateo," he said with false friendliness. "You're just in time to congratulate me. I'll be providing the meat for all these folks while they're here."

He shook hands with the Hollywood man, who mumbled a farewell and hurried back for the shade.

Bo's smile turned nasty. "This deal I just made—that's big thinking, and it brings in big money. The big thinkers are the ones who are going to survive out here long after the rest of you have skedaddled."

I glared. Bo was after our homestead, but he wasn't going to get it. Not as long as I had breath in my lungs. Bo tipped his hat to me and turned to walk away. Victor stood so Bo had to bump his shoulder to get by, and Victor bumped him back hard. Nevertheless, Bo whistled a cheerful tune as he went.

"I'd like to lay him out flat with a bloody nose," Victor murmured to me. "I still think he's the one who shot my Jenny's engine."

I nodded. We couldn't prove Bo had been working with the bootleggers, but we all suspected it. Bo would do anything to get ahead.

I took a deep breath to clear my head of Bo Young. "Let's go."

Victor took my arm and escorted me into the food tent. There was a kitchen set up in the back with several coal-fired stoves and basins with water for washing. A line of tables in front of the stoves did duty as a serving area, with other tables scattered about the tent for eating. The scents of sausage, eggs, and pancakes filled the tent.

The other ladies working on food seemed a little too happy to see Victor—especially Sytha Chamberlain. She always flirted with Victor when he was in town. The girls from Kanab gave me appraising looks that said they didn't think I would measure up—or they wondered why Victor was bothering with me—but they agreed that they could use someone else to help. I had my in. I would earn money to help my family and be able to write about the goings on at the movie scene.

CHAPTER FOUR

The silver screen might be glamorous, but after a couple of days, it was clear that cooking for the Hollywood folks was just like cooking for anyone else. If I dared bring my camera in with me, I could have snapped pictures of gorgeous Hollywood stars with sauce on their shirts or lettuce between their teeth. But I didn't think those were the kinds of photos Barry would want. So, I watched and listened instead.

Fritz Porter stepped into the tent that served as a mess hall for the crew. He wore his blond hair slicked and pomaded into a style that even the Utah wind couldn't move.

"The line is over here!" he beckoned. "Everyone eat up. The next scene is supposed to be lively. A fiesta. I don't want anyone looking lethargic."

Director, no mistaking it.

Extras shuffled past him dressed in old-fashioned clothes. It was funny to see the men with heavy greasepaint

on their faces and hands and their dark eyebrows painted on
—especially men I was used to seeing around town or at
church. The make-up wouldn't show up on the screen, of
course, but it made their eyes stand out, their skin too pale.

Some of the locals spoke to me with a sense of
conspiratorial, "We're on the same side" attitude—locals
versus Hollywood—while others seemed almost smirky that
they were acting and I wasn't. I would be smirking later
when they had to stand around in the hot sun and I took a
break in the shade.

Javi bounded up to the serving tables. He wore make-up,
too, under his poncho and sombrero. I chuckled.

"What's wrong, sis? Jealous that I look prettier than
you?" Then he paled. "Wait, no... I'm sorry you didn't get a
part, too."

I waved off his words with a spatula. "It's kind of fun to
watch everything going on behind the scenes, and I don't
have to look silly."

Javi laughed and stuck out his tongue. He beckoned over
another of the vaqueros—a brown-skinned man with the
strong nose and chin I associated with the Navajo.

"Tenny, this is Rick Yazzie. He came to Hollywood from
Shiprock, New Mexico, and now he's a big star."

Rick grinned. "Well, every time they need an Indian, they
call me. I've played plenty of Sioux, but never a Navajo, and
now I'm Mexican. That's Hollywood for you!"

"You must still enjoy it if you're staying around," I said.

Rick shrugged. "Sure, it's fun. Creative. Plus, it irks me
when people say that the Indians are vanishing." He held out
his hands. "Looks to me like we're still here, and we've still

got things to say, but no one can hear us from the reservation. So, I left home to help make home stronger."

A jolt ran up my spine. Hadn't that been why I'd gone to France, too?

Before I could respond, Victor sauntered up behind them. "What's on the menu today, Dollface?"

I raised an eyebrow. "Chicken and mashed potatoes." I lowered my voice, but included Javi and Rick in my secret. "The cake might look good, but it's as dry as dirt. You should skip it."

"Thanks for the tip. I knew you liked me." Victor waggled his eyebrows. "How about some extra mashed potatoes to make up for it?"

I pursed my lips and plopped the mashed potatoes onto his plate—the same amount as everyone else.

"Ouch!" he said. "Someday, I'll convince you that you love me."

I laughed and shook my head. Sytha and a couple of the other kitchen girls cast me curious or jealous looks. I wanted to roll my eyes at them. Couldn't they see he was a flirt? He probably would have tried the same routine with any of them if they were doling out mashed potatoes. I did notice that Victor skipped the cake, though. Good choice.

A couple of the writers came through, deep in conversation. They were along so they could advise the director and help with any last-minute scene adjustments. This was more vacation than work for them. They accepted their food politely, hardly looking at me.

"We should head down to the Grand Canyon," one of the writers said. "I've heard it's inspiring."

"That pilot is selling rides around the canyons up here."

This was working out well for Victor. And I'd spotted the Parry brothers hobnobbing with the Hollywood crowd. They were certainly drumming up a lot of business for Kane County. I hoped it paid off and kept our little community alive. Pahreah was down to just a few families at this point.

No one missed it when Johnny Fletch walked into the room. He made sure of that. He arrived late, of course. His red and white striped suit jarred horribly with the old-fashioned clothes in the tent. A cigarette dangled from his lips, and the leading lady, Thea Dove, dangled from his arm—Victor's blonde passenger. She was tall and curvy, her hair unnaturally light, and her huge, dark liquid eyes made even more so by heavy kohl.

When they reached the food counter, Thea scrunched up her pretty little nose at our lunch.

"Is there a lot of garlic in that?" she asked.

"Some in the potatoes," I said.

She turned to Johnny. "You'd better not eat any of the potatoes. We have that scene later where you try to kiss me, and I don't want to smell garlic breath."

He smirked down at her. "Baby, I'll kiss you whenever I want, and I'll do it after chomping on garlic cloves if it makes me happy. You know you like it when I show you I'm in charge." He glanced at me dismissively. "Load up my plate."

I complied—with a sympathetic look at Thea. She huffed and tore her arm away from Johnny's. Pausing long enough to grab a plate of chicken, she stormed across the room.

"I'll be skipping the mashed potatoes," said a voice behind Johnny. Elton Fairchild. He was the one playing

Zorro. Dark-haired, handsome, and with a deep, rumbling voice that made it a shame no one would hear him speak. Elton smiled at Johnny. "After all, I'm the one who'll actually be kissing Thea."

"Only on screen." Johnny's lips curled back. "You must have bribed Fritz to get the part away from me. We both know I'm the better actor. But off-screen, Thea won't be kissing anyone but me—and that's what counts. Am I right?" he asked the room in general.

People glanced away, focused on their plates. Thea looked daggers at Johnny from across the room.

Johnny laughed as if the unwilling audience were enjoying his display, then he strutted off with his lunch.

Elton rolled his eyes, then gave me a wink. "No mashed potatoes for me, please."

He even said thank you when I handed him his plate. I noticed the long look he gave Thea as he strolled past her table. She glanced his way, then turned back to pick at her fried chicken.

Ginny came in late, after we'd just started cleaning up.

"Do you have anything left?" she asked.

"There's still some chicken. And cake, but it's not very good."

"I wish you would have warned me," came Elton's deep voice.

We both turned to find him smiling at Ginny. He winked at me again. "You're absolutely right. That cake was awful. You willing to give me the inside scoop in the future?"

I felt myself blush under his grin and laughed. "Sure, Mr. Fairchild."

"Call me Elton. Any friend of Miss Hamblin's is a friend of mine. I think she's got a promising career in Hollywood ahead of her."

Ginny waved away the compliment, while Elton went on to flirt with her. My smile faded, and a cold feeling settled in my gut. I wasn't just going to lose Javi to Hollywood. I was going to lose Ginny, too. And Victor was already gone. Not that Victor had ever been mine.

"Excuse me," I mumbled, and I hurried to the back to start scrubbing up. I put plenty of elbow grease into those pots, working too ferociously to allow myself to feel bad.

"Psst! Tenny!"

I looked up to see Barry motioning to me. I sighed and dropped the scrub brush, wiping my hands dry. "Hi, Barry. How's it going?"

He groaned. "I've never seen a newsworthy event with so little news going on. I can do a write-up on all the locals getting jobs here, and that will be great, but that's not going to sell a lot of papers."

I considered that. "The Parry brothers are also leveraging this to get people to visit some of the local sites. The Grand Canyon. Maybe Bryce's Canyon. There could be a story there."

Barry nodded. "Yeah. I like your instincts. Do you think Miss Grace will have anything to tell us? You're getting an inside scoop here."

I hesitated and looked back at the pile of dishes. "Look, Barry, I could talk about how the Hollywood folks are just like us, but I don't want to run a gossip column. It feels dirty. Besides, there's not much to gossip about." It didn't feel right to talk about the competition between Elton and Johnny over Thea or the roles in the movie.

He looked deflated. "Well, do the best you can. If we can't get people interested in our stories, we may lose the paper. That's going to hurt both of us."

I nodded. It would. My family needed that income. It might be a sign that Kane County was dying, and all of us would go our separate ways. "I'll see what I can do."

Barry accepted that and left. I went to dump out the dirty dish water in the back. The water sloshed over the red dirt, which quickly sucked it up. Thirsty for anything that would help keep it alive.

Two voices came to me from somewhere beyond the food tent.

Two angry voices.

I should just walk away. It wasn't my business. People had arguments all the time.

But I couldn't help thinking about what Barry had said. What if there was some kind of story here? I didn't want to turn to nasty gossip, but I had to find something to write about that would keep the paper and Miss Grace in circulation. I crept closer, trying to tell who was speaking, at least.

One of the voices was too quiet to hear, but the other was unmistakable: Johnny Fletch.

"I don't care how you *feel*. Neither of us is getting out of this now. We're in too deep."

A mumbled reply.

"Oh, so this is my fault? No, your hands are just as dirty as mine."

I still couldn't hear the reply. Was he talking to Thea? Another actor? I wasn't certain I wanted to know what kind of dirty deal they might have made.

"I don't need to threaten you. You're the one threatening me with your talk of backing out. We see this out together or we go down together—do you understand?"

I ducked out of sight as someone stomped by. The quiet crunch of a second set of footsteps went off in the other direction. When I thought it was safe, I looked out. No one was left. Whatever that was about, there certainly were some nasty Hollywood secrets here on the movie set. Gossip people might be interested in. But what should I do with it?

CHAPTER FIVE

Later that evening, I sat at my typewriter, staring at the bleak white of the blank page, trying to find something to say about the movie set that didn't make me feel dirty. My eyes burned with weariness, and I had to get up early to cook, but we needed to keep people interested in the movie. It was good for the paper. It was good for Kane County. People might love to hear about Johnny Fletch's backstage dealings, but that would make the movie look bad and discourage Hollywood from bringing more work here. Part of me wanted that. Wanted to be able to survive without them. But I didn't know if we could.

So, upbeat gossip. Keep Kane County happy and keep Hollywood happy. Elton Fairchild's smile flashed in my mind. I grinned to myself. Yes, there was something positive. Everyone would probably like to hear that Zorro, the star of the show, was as charming off-screen as on. A win for everyone.

I began typing, filling the quiet with the satisfying click of the keys under my fingers, the staccato rhythm of the typeheads hitting the ribbon, the ding of the margin bell warning me I'd come to the end of the line. Papa had his salterio and Javi had his guitar, but this was my music, dancing across the page and filling the emptiness with ideas.

A tap on the door interrupted my rhythm. Daisy raised her head and barked. I groaned. Papa was clearing a ditch outside, Rosie was out with Mel, and Mother and Abuela were taking stock of the root cellar.

"Javi!" I called.

Nothing. He'd snuck off somewhere again. He was a little young to be serious about girls, and he knew better than to go looking for a speakeasy. What was he up to?

I sighed and left my typewriter to answer the door. Victor stood there, leaning against the door frame and grinning at me.

"Hey, Doll. Thought I'd drop by for a visit. If I may?"

"Of course. Everyone else is out, though."

His smile brightened. "That's all right. I can catch up with them later. I'd rather talk to you anyway."

"Oh." My cheeks warmed. We'd had a few serious conversations when he'd flown through before, but I felt a sort of nervous uncertainty as I let him in. At least, I thought that was why my heart was beating so fast.

Victor circled the room, pausing to admire my collection of petrified wood. He whistled when he saw my photographs of ancient, twisted juniper trees in the canyons—survivors in the face of brutal conditions. Mother had arranged the little rectangles in a frame on the wall, declaring them worthy of display, but a wave of bashfulness washed over me at Victor's interest.

"You've got an eye for this," he said.

"I hope so. It might help the paper. If we can keep it open, anyway."

"It's that bad, huh?" He turned his full attention to me, eyes full of sympathy.

"Maybe. People here are struggling. This movie could be a big thing for us. Thank you for helping with it."

"Well, the Parry brothers deserve most of the credit. I just hope they do a war movie out here so I can be in one of the pictures."

"I thought you were doing movies in California."

"Sure, a few. But I get antsy if I can't move around." He lowered his voice. "And I'd like to spend more time here."

"Really, here?"

He smiled a little. "Sure. Haven't you caught on to that?"

My face heated, and I looked down, away, everywhere but at him. Was he still just flirting, or did he mean it?

He pointed to the camera on my desk. "What else are you working on?"

I hesitated. He'd figured out my identity as Miss Grace during the bootlegging incident. Even though I couldn't always read his intentions, I didn't mind that he knew my secret. He didn't mock me over it, and I didn't have a lot of other people I could talk to about my writing—just my family and Ginny.

"More pictures of the desert," I said. "And Javi found this place in one of the canyons. Have you heard of Cliff Palace out in Colorado?"

"Oh, the ruins? Sure, I've heard of them." His eyes brightened with interest. "Say, your brother found something like that?"

"Not as big, but it's undisturbed. That's the problem, though. I want to write something about it, but I don't want it to be ruined."

"Outsiders will do that, won't they?" Victor said a little wryly.

"Some of them might. Locals, too. I want to tell people about it but also protect it. I would hate to make money by destroying something amazing."

He smiled and took my hand. I didn't pull away. His grip was strong and comforting. "I'm sure you'll do the right thing." His gaze fell on the typewriter. "Is that what you're working on now? I'd love to see it. If you'd trust me with it."

"I think I would, but I haven't decided what to write about that yet."

"Ah, Miss Grace, then."

"I'm still answering letters," I said, "but I'd like to write about more. It would help the newspaper, and my family could use the extra money."

"Your devotion to family is admirable, but what about you? Do you like doing this for yourself, too?"

His question caught me off guard. I'd never stopped to think about it that way before. But the answer was easy. "I do! I like feeling useful, and I enjoy... well, having little puzzles to solve, figuring out the best way to express an idea."

He smiled. "Then I think it's great that you're doing it. So, what problem is Miss Grace tackling today?"

He glanced down at the sheet in the typewriter. I almost jumped in to cover the words. It felt vulnerable to let someone see what I'd written before I'd had a chance to edit it. But I was also proud of what I'd come up with.

"I didn't want to write regular gossip about the movie," I said. "It feels cheap. So I thought I'd take a positive spin on Hollywood being here."

His smile faded as he read.

"Don't you like it?" I asked.

"I didn't know you were such an Elton Fairchild fan. You like his movies, I suppose."

"He seems very kind. He was giving Ginny acting tips."

"I bet he was! A Hollywood smile and a few nonsensical words to a pretty woman, and now he's kind."

I flushed. I needed this to be a good story, not just a girl gushing about a handsome star. Was that how it sounded? "He talks to me—to everyone—like a regular person. Down-to-earth. Not like Johnny Fletch."

"Ha! Everyone's a saint compared to Johnny Fletch! But I wouldn't put Elton Fairchild on a very high pedestal either."

"I'm not putting him on a pedestal. I just need something to write about. Something upbeat. Kane County needs it."

"And he's the best you could do?" Victor snapped.

I balled my fists. "Yes, I suppose he is!"

"Well, good luck to you. I hope you have a fine evening daydreaming about Elton Fairchild."

He turned and stomped out the front door just as the kitchen door squeaked opened.

"What was that about?" Mother called.

I tore the paper from the typewriter and crumpled it. "It was nothing, Mother."

CHAPTER SIX

I showed up at the set the next morning with a half-hearted article for Barry about the behind-the-scenes work on the movie. The locals would be happy to see their contributions acknowledged, but I didn't think it would really grab their attention. Between Victor's reaction to my article and my own doubts about what I should write, my words had come out stiff and emotionless.

Mel Young lurked behind the food tent, peeking through the flaps and ducking out of sight again. He had a job helping to build the sets, but I hadn't seen him around the food tent before.

I stuffed my article in my apron pocket. "Morning, Mel," I said in a low voice.

He gave a start and turned with a sheepish grin. "Hi, Tenny," he whispered.

"Are you looking for Rosie?"

"Yes, but I don't want my father to know I'm here." He

adjusted the glasses that held on his tin mask. "I'm sorry. That must sound awful. Rosie's amazing. I'm lucky she... she'll have anything to do with me. But my father's on the set today, and he..."

I put a hand on his arm. "I know. I understand. And she's lucky to have you as well. You're a swell guy. Good luck lying low."

But as I scrambled eggs for breakfast, I heard Bo's booming voice outside the tent.

"What are you doing here? Following that Mateo girl around like a puppy?"

"I'm here to support her," Mel said. "I like her, and she likes me. The Mateos are good people. Why can't you leave them alone?"

"Why can't you get it through your thick head that I'm looking out for you? Farming in Kane County ain't easy. We need more land. More water. We were here before the Mateos, and their land ought to be ours."

"But they homesteaded it and worked it."

"We used to run our cattle there. That ought to count for something. Look, my father was a lazy drunk. He left me with nothing. I had to start from scratch, building all this up. And I'm going to keep building it until I have a real legacy to leave behind. A real legacy for you."

"Legacies are about more than property," Mel grumbled.

"What's that supposed to mean? Haven't I taught you to be strong? To squeeze every resource out of what we have? That's a legacy—survival. Working against the odds and winning."

"You have taught me to work hard," Mel acknowledged.

"I appreciate that lesson. But I don't want to win at whatever cost."

Bo snorted. "You'll learn. It's survival of the fittest—winner takes all. There's no room for the losers out here in the desert."

Footsteps retreated—Mel's or Bo's, I didn't know, and I certainly wasn't going to peek.

Bo's statements left me in a thoughtful mood. He was looking out for his family, just like I was. Not that I would do the things he had done to get ahead, but what if he was right that Kane County was just not big enough for everyone to succeed? I brushed my hands off on my apron, not in the mood for any kind of gossip. The other girls seemed to sense that and gave me space, though that meant they were now whispering about me.

I ignored them.

Javi and Rick Yazzie came in to get an early breakfast. This morning, their vaquero costumes struck me as especially silly. Who really dressed like that? Not anyone in Mexico. Hollywood. It was all fake, and it brewed a sour feeling in my stomach.

Johnny Fletch swaggered in and cut in front of Javi and Rick. "Make way for someone who has some real work to do today." Johnny laughed. "A couple of no-good Mexicans can wait for their food."

Sytha Chamberlain's mouth fell open in shock. Several heads turned Johnny's way, then quickly found somewhere else to look. A stiff quiet fell over the tent.

"What did you say?" Javi said, balling his hands into fists.

Johnny laughed. "Don't get so hot under the collar. I'm just playing my part."

Javi took a step forward, but Johnny's face grew hard and red. "Don't even think about it. You think the director cares about either of you? You mess with me, and you're gone."

Rick put a hand on Javi's arm and shook his head. Javi glared at Johnny.

I wanted to spit in Johnny's food, but I didn't. Instead, I shoved the plate in his direction and hurried to get the next plates ready for Javi and Rick.

They took their food with mumbled thanks.

I still felt hot and sick by the time Ginny arrived, dressed in her "Spanish lady" costume, with its flouncy skirt and bows on the sleeve. Not very Spanish. But Ginny was pale beneath her make-up.

"Are you all right?" I whispered as I dished up her lunch.

"I'm not sure I can do this, Tenny," she whispered. "I have my big scene today. I have to faint. I never was a fainter."

I tried to smile. "That's why it's acting."

"I know. And Elton gave me some pointers, but I'm so nervous. Do you think you can come watch? You know, cheer me on?"

Sure, I could go watch my friend make her big break and leave Utah behind for the mirage that was Hollywood. But this was important to her, so I nodded. "I'll be there."

During cleanup, I hung up my apron and slipped out to find where they were shooting. They had a roofless hacienda set up with stairs going to a second floor landing and doors in the back that led nowhere but a narrow walkway and the timber frame holding the whole thing together—though the audience wouldn't see anything but what the director wanted them to see.

This was a big sword fight scene, where Zorro rescued the señoritas in distress. They even had musicians playing off to the side to create the atmosphere, a piano sitting out there in the desert.

Bo Young was standing around looking like the cat that ate the canary. I stayed as far from him as I could and watched Fritz Porter set the scene.

I was surprised to see Sam Ellis standing to the side with his arms folded and a scowl on his face. I made my way over to him and nodded a greeting.

"Watching the show?" I asked. "I didn't think you wanted anything to do with Hollywood."

He gave me a rueful smile and gestured with his head toward Ginny. "I don't, but she does. She had me watch her practice fainting a few dozen times last night, so I thought I'd come to see how the real thing went."

Sam watched Ginny with thinly-veiled admiration. What an odd relationship they had. Ginny had no interest in settling down—and a relationship between a white woman and a Paiute man would no doubt be frowned on, even though it wasn't technically illegal in Utah—yet she and Sam were undeniably close. Would Hollywood lure her away from her homestead and from her friends here? The nervous excitement lighting her face as she waited for the camera to start rolling made my stomach feel heavy.

The cameraman glanced over at me. "Hey, you're Victor Holbrook's friend, aren't you?"

"I'm his friend, yes," I said, wondering how this stranger knew.

"He took me out for a ride on his plane and mentioned that you're a photographer—pointed you out to me when we got back. Said you have some film to develop with some impressive pictures?"

"Oh, that was kind of him." It really was. I wondered if this was before or after our argument of the night before.

"I can help you develop it so you don't have to send it away," the cameraman said. "I'm Willis."

"Thank you! That would be wonderful. I'm Tenny Mateo."

Willis nodded. Before we could say anything else, Fritz called action, and Willis had to focus on his camera.

The musicians played a fast-paced ragtime tune. It didn't fit the movie, but the audience wouldn't hear it; it just kept the energy high for the scene.

Ginny was sitting near Thea, pretending to gossip. Johnny burst into the "room" with the gang of vaqueros, including Javi and Rick, and he grabbed Thea.

Ginny shrieked and fell into a swoon. It looked real. She did have a knack for this.

Johnny ran up the stairs, dragging Thea with him.

Elton, as Zorro, rushed into the scene. He helped Ginny to her feet, then chased Johnny and Thea up the stairs.

Javi played his role in the fight, getting in Elton's way and taking a punch. The punch wasn't real, but Javi made a genuine tumble down the stairs—doing his own stunts. I winced when he landed. I could tell it hurt by the look on his face, but he stumbled to his feet and fled the "hacienda."

After some flashy swordplay from Elton, Rick and the other vaqueros followed.

Johnny shoved Thea through one of the doors that went nowhere but behind the set. He turned back to draw his sword and fight Elton. The choreographer shouted reminders to them as they fought. The clanging of the foils seemed real enough. I gasped when Johnny disarmed Elton, even though I knew there was no real danger. Elton rushed in, and they grappled. Thea stepped into the doorframe and hit Johnny with a vase. It shattered over his head, as it was designed to do, and Elton pushed him back through the doorway.

Elton and Thea found a moment to embrace on the landing. They exchanged some nonsense drowned out by the ragtime music and Fritz's shouted instruction. It would be covered later with heroic dialogue on the screen.

Then Elton and Thea stood there, the embrace turning silly and awkward while they waited to be interrupted.

"Johnny?" Fritz called up the stairs.

Johnny stumbled through the doorway. From the front, it all looked so real. He clutched his side, his face pale and pained. I had to admit, for everything else about him, he was a good actor. He pushed past Thea and Elton and collapsed at the top of the stairs.

"Cut!" Fritz called.

The music stopped, and everyone relaxed.

"That was great, everyone," Fritz said, "but Johnny, you're not supposed to fall until Elton hits you again."

Ginny walked over to me. "That was fun," she whispered.

"You're a natural," I said. "The only person whose acting was better was Johnny."

We glanced over to where he was slumped at the top of the stairs. I rolled my eyes. What a ham.

"All right, Johnny," Elton called. "We're all impressed."

Johnny didn't move.

The director clapped his hands. "We need to set up the scene again."

Still no movement.

Ginny and I exchanged worried looks. My nurse's training kicked in, and I ran up the stairs. Johnny lay curled up on his side. I touched his shoulder. It rested at an awkward angle. Had he been hurt in the fight?

"Mr. Fletch?" I asked. "Are you injured?"

Nothing.

I rolled him over. A bright red stain bloomed across his shirt. I grabbed his wrist. No pulse. His face had a pale, empty look I recognized too well.

Fritz rushed up behind me. "What is this? A stunt? Knock it off!"

He knelt down to shake Johnny.

I tried to stop him. "I don't think you should—"

Fritz pulled his hand away, staring at the sticky blood dampening his fingers.

Ginny drew a sharp breath behind me.

"—touch him until we call the sheriff," I finished.

"Johnny!" Thea screamed. She stepped forward, eyes wide, hand extended. Then she fainted into a heap on the floor.

I thought Ginny had done it better.

Fritz wiped a shaky hand on his pants and rolled his eyes at Thea. He probably shouldn't have been so irreverent with a dead man on the floor, but Thea was going to be in the way when Sheriff Moore showed up.

Most people were too busy staring in shock or running around doing pointless things to pay much attention to Thea, but Elton was pretty quick to come to her side.

"Nobody leave the set!" Fritz called. He pointed at my new friend Willis. "Except you. Go get the sheriff."

From my vantage on the stairs, I scanned the stunned faces on the set. Fritz paced. Ginny looked ill. One of the writers stepped up to guard Willis's camera—and rightly so, since it might provide evidence. Javi and the other vaqueros were gone. And so were Sam Ellis and Bo Young.

Sheriff Moore didn't take long getting there, and when he did, Thea was still sprawled on the upstairs floor with Elton comforting her.

"Did the attacker go after the lady, too?" Sheriff Moore asked.

I shook my head. "She was overcome by the shock."

The sheriff glared at her and Elton. "Get her out of here, then. I don't need dramatics around a crime scene. But don't go far. I'll have questions for everyone who was here."

Thea looked torn between disappointment that she had to leave and excitement for the attention coming later. I was sure she'd have a very dramatic account for the sheriff. He was going to hate it.

Sheriff Moore looked over the body then stood and glanced around the set at everyone present. "All right. What happened?"

When everyone stared blankly, he sighed and turned to me. "Hortencia Mateo. What did you see?"

I cleared my throat. "Johnny went out onto the platforms behind the set." I pointed to the door. "He was late coming back, and when he did, he stumbled in and collapsed."

Sheriff Moore looked through the false doorway at the platforms and stairs behind the set. Peeking through, I could see the bloodstain on the wood.

"He walked back there?" Sheriff Moore asked, nudging part of the broken vase with his foot. "It was part of the script?"

I shifted. "Well, Thea Dove hit him over the head with a vase and Elton pushed him back there—that was scripted."

Fritz nodded. "We all thought it was part of the scene when he collapsed. It wasn't until everything was over that we knew something was wrong."

"A man died in front of you, and none of you knew what was happening?" Sheriff Moore glared at everyone.

Most of them looked shocked or abashed. But I did feel guilty. I had seen men die in the battlefield hospitals in France. I should have recognized death. The initial fight for life, followed by the slow fading as the person lets go, the moorings holding body and soul together wear thin, and then that spark snuffs out all at once, and in that moment, everything changes: they are forever, unalterably gone from anywhere that we can reach them.

"He always was an excellent actor," the director said quietly.

We all stared at the body on the floor, all its potential gone.

"Who knew he was in this scene?" the sheriff asked.

The director shook his head like he was trying to clear his mind of what he'd witnessed. "Well, everyone knew."

Sheriff Moore nodded. "All right. I'll need statements from everyone. Be prepared to provide witnesses confirming where you were just before and during this scene. I'm bringing in a doctor to see what he can tell me about the stab wound."

We all wandered out of the set, dazed. Ginny came up beside me, put an arm around my shoulder. Neither of us said anything, just stared out over the red desert.

CHAPTER SEVEN

J avi ran up, panting. "Ten, is it true? Is Johnny dead?"

He looked frightened. Of course, he and Johnny had a public disagreement just that morning, and he wasn't in the scene when Johnny died. It would look bad for Javi. And he was always sneaking around. Could anyone verify where he'd been? Would anyone? I knew my brother wouldn't stab anyone. Hopefully, the sheriff knew that too.

"It's true," I said slowly. "How did you hear?"

"Thea is practically shouting about it to anyone who will listen." He made a face. "Honestly, I didn't believe her."

"This time, at least, she's telling the truth. Where did you go after you left the set?"

He hesitated.

I pushed forward. "Javi, the sheriff is going to want to know. He's going to talk to everyone."

"Don't worry! I'll talk to him." He shrugged me off and walked away.

Victor cut his way through the milling crowd, looking confused at the chaos.

"What's the fuss, Miss Mateo?" he asked.

I turned to face him, my rancor from the night before forgotten. Where had he been this morning? Not that I thought he would murder anyone—not even Bo Young, much as he disliked our belligerent neighbor. "Someone was killed on set."

Victor's forehead wrinkled. "An accident?"

I shook my head. "Murder. Johnny Fletch was murdered. The sheriff is investigating."

Victor whistled.

I gave him a pointed look. "You'll have to talk to him."

He smiled ruefully. "Won't that be a pleasure for both of us? Don't worry, Doll. I've got nothing to hide this time. I went straight, remember? Besides, I've been flying, so this time, the sheriff can't pin it on me."

I tried to smile back. I was glad Victor was in the clear, but that didn't change the fact that there was a murderer on the loose in Kane County.

The doctor's wagon rattled past. Not long after, it creaked away again, this time with a wrapped figure in the back. I let out a slow breath and watched it go.

Sheriff Moore caught my eye and gestured for me to follow him. Ginny gave my arm a squeeze, and Victor offered me an encouraging smile. I couldn't bring myself to smile back, just nodded and scurried after the sheriff.

He led me to a room in the ranch house—his makeshift office on the set now, I guessed.

"So," Sheriff Moore drawled, pointing for me to sit across from him. "I've already heard the director's version of events. Let's hear what you have to say, since you're all mixed up in this."

"I'm not mixed up in it," I said, a little defensive. "I was just a witness. And, I may have heard something important."

He sighed heavily. "Let's hear it."

I told him about Johnny's argument I'd overheard the previous day.

The sheriff chewed at the end of his mustache. "The person he was arguing with, could it have been a woman?"

"Yes. The voice seemed low, but it could have been a woman trying not to be overheard."

"And the deceased threatened the person?"

The deceased. Johnny Fletch. I drew a deep breath. "He threatened to take them down with him."

"From what you've seen on the set, who might Mr. Fletch threaten?"

"Honestly? Almost anyone. He was not a likable person."

"So I've gathered. Did you see anyone in particular he didn't get along with? And don't say 'everyone.'"

I grinned sheepishly then grew serious again. Johnny had been an awful person, but that didn't mean he deserved to die. "Well, he bullied around Thea Dove. And..." I sighed, hating to tattle on anyone. "And he and Elton Fairchild had been arguing."

Sheriff Moore nodded as if he already knew this. Did he

know that Johnny had been bullying Javi, too? It didn't matter. Javi fell into the category of "everyone," including me. I was only mentioning people who might have a real motive.

"Do you know of anything that he might have blackmailed anyone over?"

My eyes widened. "Blackmail?" I paused to think about it. People on the set no doubt had secrets. "He seems like the type who might do it, but I don't know to whom."

"Did you hear anything at the time he was stabbed? A call for help, maybe?"

Good question. Most people did not die quietly. "No. It was loud on the set. There was a piano playing ragtime and people talking. If he shouted, I couldn't hear it."

"But Miss Dove and Mr. Fairchild were the closest to him."

"Yes," I said slowly. They might have been able to hear if Johnny said anything in his final moments.

"From your angle, do you think either of them had the opportunity to attack Mr. Fletch?"

"It was a fight scene." I remember Javi taking that punch and rolling down the stairs. "They might have been able to hurt him for real and make it look like part of the show." Especially if they had been working together.

"Okay." Sheriff Moore sighed again and rubbed his eyes. "That's all for now. You can send in the next person. Don't leave town, though I imagine you're not planning on it."

He said that with a bit of a snicker. Well, I didn't plan to go anywhere at the moment, but had he forgotten that I'd been born in the Mormon colonies in Mexico? Gone to Dixie College? Been a nurse in France? It wasn't like I never went anywhere. I just didn't want to see my family and our haven here fall apart.

I opened the door to find Thea and Elton waiting outside. Their faces were stormy, and I caught Thea's last words.

"If you don't say something, I will!"

I stared at them, and they stared back, all of us with various levels of embarrassment and uncertainty.

Then the sheriff called, "Who's next?"

I hurried away. Let Sheriff Moore sort it out. He wasn't going to be able to say that I was interfering this time.

In the food tent, I found a group of frazzled cast members and set workers standing around with soda bottles or coffees. Sytha was sidled up to Victor, listening with wide eyes.

Victor laughed. "I've been through this before. If you didn't do anything wrong, you've got nothing to worry about."

Ginny shook her head. "I've been through it, too, and I don't need to relive that."

"At least you couldn't have done it," a make-up girl, Jane, said. "You were on stage when he... when it..." She looked green.

I grabbed her a soda bottle with a sympathetic smile. She took it, her hands a little shaky. "Thanks. I don't have any idea what happened, but just thinking about talking to the sheriff makes me feel guilty."

"You'll be fine," I told her.

One of the writers, a man with slicked-back blond hair and a crumpled suit, held a coffee with both hands like he was cold despite the desert heat. "I hope so. This is such a mess. Is it possible the killer will strike again?"

That brought a hush to the group. Leave it to a writer to jump to worst-case scenario.

Victor shook his head. "Stick to scaring us on the screen, Lloyd. It will be something personal, just watch. Let's be honest, no one liked Johnny Fletch. He finally pushed someone too far. Nothing for the rest of us to worry about."

There were some mumbles of agreement from the group. Johnny wasn't going to be missed, unless it interfered with the movie schedule, and even then, he'd played his final scene. Final scene ever.

Victor must have noticed my frown. He made his way past Jane's admiring glance to stand by me. I felt my cheeks warm a little.

"You thinking about writing this up?" he said in a low voice. "It's your big news story. Everyone will buy the paper now."

I sighed. "Part of me would like to, but I'm sure Barry will take this one. I didn't even bring my camera to the set." I glanced up at him. "Thank you, by the way, for talking to Willis for me."

"You should get your pictures out there for people to see. And maybe you should keep your camera handy on the set from now on."

"I thought you said we didn't need to worry."

"I might have lied a little to make people feel better. There's a killer walking around."

"And he'd like his picture taken?"

Victor's lips turned up in a half-smile. "He or she. But you can't tell me you don't want to write about this."

I sighed. How had he learned to read me so well? "I might do an opinion piece about how everyone deserves justice. I'd written something about the locals working on the set, but no one will want to read that now."

He looked thoughtful. "Johnny must have had *some* redeeming qualities. Maybe you could find out what they were."

I groaned. "A difficult task, but not a bad idea. Any ideas where I should start?"

"We all know he was a good actor. And he seemed to really get into his role. He asked me a lot about the area. Even wanted to take a plane ride to get to know it better. I feel a bit badly now that he never got to."

We stood in silence for a moment, mourning someone who was difficult to mourn. But Victor was right. This wouldn't be over until the murderer was found.

CHAPTER EIGHT

E ven in scandal-ridden Hollywood, murder was shocking enough to shut down the set for a few days while the sheriff interviewed witnesses and everyone came to terms with Johnny's death. Barry splashed the news all over the paper, and I imagined curious locals sneaking around the quiet set to gawk at the site of the tragedy. I stayed home. There was something soothing about the normalcy of plucking weeds from between rows of potatoes and cabbages. At the end of each row, I could look back and see that I had accomplished something orderly and uncomplicated.

The buzz of Victor's plane approaching didn't surprise me. I dealt with the trauma of war and death by lying low, while he tried to dodge it by always moving, yet everyone sometimes needs a solid place to land. Our house was the closest Victor had to home in southern Utah.

I dusted the red dirt from my gloves and walked over to greet Victor.

"The movie's starting back up tomorrow," he told me. "I wanted to make sure you knew."

"Thank you. And you'll want to stay for dinner, of course."

"Of course!" He grinned, but it faded quickly. "Have you thought about what to write for the paper? Everyone in town is talking about the murder."

I hesitated, remembering Victor's reaction to my story about Elton.

He seemed to read my face. Or my heart. "Look, I'm sorry about how I reacted to your article about Fairchild. It was good. That was the problem. I don't want you falling under the spell of these Hollywood phonies."

"You really think I would?"

"I probably shouldn't. I haven't managed to get you under my spell, and look how charming I am."

"Ha!"

He grabbed my hand, his strong, warm fingers pressing mine and sending an electric shiver up my arm. "See, that's why I'm jealous. What if one of them gets to you first?"

"No one's going to 'get to' me," I lied.

Because I was afraid Victor already had. I never knew if I could trust his flirting, but the intense look he gave me at the moment, his gaze traveling my face, resting on my lips, made me feel like everything inside of me had turned to feathers, fluttering around and putting me in danger of floating away.

"That would be a shame," Victor said, his voice a low rumble. "But it's not going to stop me from trying."

He reached out and brushed my short hair back from my face, tucking it behind my ear. I stared at him, not able to move and not wanting to.

"Javi!" Papa's voice shattered the moment.

I jumped back from Victor, and he tucked his hands behind his back.

Papa came out from the barn, his normally cheerful expression dark. "Have either of you seen Javi?"

I shook my head quickly, my pulse racing. "I haven't. Not since breakfast. I thought he was helping you. Uh, getting one of the fields ready. The cornfield, maybe?"

Victor gave me an amused look, and I flushed. I was talking too fast, sounding guilty. Why did I feel guilty?

Luckily, Papa wasn't paying attention. "He was supposed to be helping me get the field ready, but he's wandered off."

That brought me back to earth. Oh, Javi. What were you doing?

Victor cleared his throat. "Maybe he's in town. Everyone is there gossiping about the murder."

Papa sighed. "This movie isn't going to help us save the homestead if there's no one left to work on it." He glanced over at the work I did. "At least I can always count on you, Hortencia."

I smiled stiffly as he walked back to the barn. Yes, he could always count on me. I wasn't going anywhere. I wasn't going to run off with Victor and fly around the country doing Hollywood stunts or barnstorming acts. I was going to stay right here and save my family.

All the feathers inside me turned to stones.

I swiveled reluctantly back to Victor. "I have been writing

something about Johnny Fletch. About remembering that everyone brings some good into the world. I'd love to hear what you think about it."

"I'd be honored. And if you use up the rest of your film, Willis can help you develop it. I bet you'll have something amazing to publish." The look he gave me was so full of understanding that I couldn't meet his eyes. I turned my back on him and led the way back to the house.

CHAPTER NINE

I headed to the set early the next morning. I dropped Miss Grace's column off to Barry, determined from there to put the Johnny Fletch investigation behind me and get my job done. Though I did bring my camera. Just in case. It felt strange to be back—everything the same but different, like a flash flood had crashed through the set.

The writers were anxious to grab their coffees and make sure the script was corrected so it didn't require Johnny's character. Just like that, he was written out of the story, and the world went on without him.

I snapped a picture of the writers hunched over their coffees and scripts.

"Are you taking pictures for the paper?" Sytha Chamberlain asked.

I turned, scrambling for an answer. Few people knew I was Miss Grace, and they might not want to read the column if they realized it was just Tenny Mateo writing it.

"I saw you talking to that newspaper man," she said.

"Uh, yes, he wanted to know more about what everyone does on set."

Sytha flipped her curled bob. "I could give him some interesting gossip."

I ground my teeth. Was she going to edge me out because my standards were higher? Was I being unreasonable?

One of the girls from Kanab sidled up to me. "If you take our picture, does that mean we might be in the paper?" Her eyes shone, and she glanced longingly at the camera.

"Sure, maybe. You want me to get a shot of you?"

"Yes, please!"

She motioned over one of her friends, all excited to pose together for a photograph. Even Sytha joined in, after a moment frowning at the scene from the side. I felt too shy to use my camera around the actors and actresses, especially with everyone on edge because of the murder, but the other behind-the-scenes workers were thrilled to have their pictures taken. They wanted proof that they'd been a part of Hollywood, especially now that it was notorious. That shouldn't have surprised me anymore. After the kitchen girls, I snapped pictures of set builders and stunt men.

"You're going to use up that roll of film in no time," Victor said, coming over to watch as I noted the names of the stunt men on the back of the film.

"I can use these pictures for the newspaper. Maybe I'll write that article about locals and behind-the-scenes workers on the set. Some of them have interesting life stories."

"Oh, yeah, like men who served in the war and now do stunts for Hollywood?" he asked too casually.

I chuckled. "Maybe something like that." I held up my camera, suddenly feeling shy. "I don't think I have a picture of you."

He grinned. "I thought you'd never ask!"

Why hadn't I asked? Victor was a handsome subject, and I didn't have any pictures of him. I couldn't pretend it was because I didn't want to remember him. Maybe I was afraid to try to capture something I didn't think I would be able to keep. Like taking a picture of the wind.

I snapped a photo of him in front of his plane, but it made something twist in my chest. That moment was there and gone, already in the past, and who knew where either of us would be when the picture was developed?

"You going to write my name in that little slot?" he asked.

"I don't think I'm likely to forget *you*." I tried to sound light-hearted, but the words came out too heavy.

He gave me a curious look and walked with me back to the food tent.

Jane, the make-up girl, approached me shyly. "Can you take my picture, too?"

"Of course!"

She smiled, though her eyes looked sad, as if she'd been crying. "I make everyone else look nice for the cameras, but I don't usually get my picture taken." Her smile crumpled. "Johnny said he was going to change that."

Victor, who had been lingering, recognized his cue to leave.

I put an arm around Jane. "I'm sorry. I didn't know you were... friends with him."

"He told me I had real talent. That I just needed to be discovered and I'd be going places. Now, I'm afraid no one will notice me."

She leaned against my shoulder, and her warm tears soaked into my dress.

I patted her awkwardly. "I'm sure if Johnny saw it, other people will, too. How about if you get dressed up, and then we take a few pictures. That will use up the last of this film."

"Oh, really? Thank you!" She dabbed at her eyes and hurried off with a weak smile.

Johnny was promising young girls a shot, was he? In exchange for what, I didn't want to know. Hopefully, Sheriff Moore was unearthing the same information.

Lloyd, the writer, approached me. "I'm glad to see you being kind to her. I'm afraid Mr. Fletch raised a lot of false expectations."

"That kind of thing is common in Hollywood, I suppose?"

He sighed and sat next to me. "I believe so. It's a nastier world than the glamour of the silver screen leads people to believe."

My stomach tightened. And this was the world taking away people I cared about. Javi. Ginny. Even Victor.

Lloyd gave me a speculative glance. "I'm surprised they didn't cast you as an extra. You have a Spanish look about you."

I nodded. "My dad's Mexican, and my Abuela is from Spain. My brother and sister got parts, but I guess I was too late. It's kind of nice to be behind the scenes. Less pressure."

"Indeed!" he said with feeling. "Not everyone enjoys the spotlight."

I raised my camera. "Do you want your picture taken anyway? To remember?"

He smiled and shook his head, the sun bright on his slicked-back blond hair. "I don't care about photographs. It's the stories I'm interested in. That's what I want people to remember."

"You must love writing for Hollywood, then."

He looked sheepish. "Well, I do. They don't always listen to my suggestions, but the big picture, at least, is still there. I wish sometimes they'd get their history right, though."

"At least Zorro isn't a true story, so they can't get it very wrong."

"It's not factual, but it still has its moments of truth," he said. "The idea of someone standing up to the people in power to give voice to the voiceless. That's a powerful idea."

"Yes, it is."

A high-pitched laugh grated on my nerves, and I looked up to see Thea flirting with Victor. My lips twisted in a frown. Why did she have to be so obnoxious about it?

"Oh, you simply must take me flying again, darling," she said in that gravely voice. "It's so *breathtaking*." She rested a hand on his chest.

I wanted to yell at her not to touch him, but it wasn't my business who he flirted with.

"Sure thing, one of these days," Victor said, not leaning into her touch, but not backing away from it, either. "But I

have a few other customers lined up before you." He nodded
to Lloyd.

She gave us a dismissive glance. "Surely, when you say
customer, you don't mean that you'd charge me this time, do
you? I thought we were friends."

He smiled. "Gas costs money. I was going to charge
Johnny, too." He looked my way again. "I only do free flights
in special cases."

Thea pulled her hand away. "And I'm not special?" Her
too-sweet smile returned. "You know, I might be able to
arrange some more work for you in Hollywood. I know
plenty of people."

"Hmm." Victor said, not rejecting her offer, but not
committing to it, either.

"Think about it," she said with a bit of a hiss and
stormed off.

Victor smiled at me. "See, Doll? You can't let these
Hollywood types take you in. Johnny complained about my
prices, too. At least Lloyd here never did."

"Fair is fair," Lloyd said. "I suppose you're doing pretty
good business?"

"Yeah, not bad at all. The Parry brothers have the right of
it: Hollywood might help Kanab, but the thing that's going
to save it is tourism. Grand Canyon, Bryce's Canyon, Zion: If
we can get the word out, this could be a booming place for
tourists. It'll help the locals, too," he added with a grin
at me.

I sighed. "I suppose it would, though it might bring its
share of trouble, too."

"It's all trouble, Sweetheart. It's just a matter of which

kind of trouble you're left with." He lowered his voice. "Speaking of which."

We glanced back to see Elton Fairchild approaching. The actor flashed a vague smile at Lloyd and I, then fixed a much brighter one on Victor.

"I understand Thea has her heart set on an airplane ride."

"I'm happy to take customers up over the valley, but I can't afford to do it for free."

"Sure, I get it. Thea's taking Johnny's death pretty hard, and I want her happy so we can finish this movie. I'll pay for her trip, and one for me as well."

"I can only take one passenger at a time," Victor cautioned.

"Oh, that's fine by me. She's a bit much to handle right now, but maybe some time in the air will calm her down." He looked Victor up and down. "You were a pilot in the war?"

Victor nodded curtly.

"Good work you fellows did over there. I was in army training when the war ended. Always felt a little guilty that I didn't get a chance to do my bit."

"At least you were willing," Victor said, still a little cool.

I could guess what he was thinking: plenty of us did go Over There to do our bit.

"Well, I'm glad we got the plane situation all figured out," Elton said, flashing another of his Hollywood grins. "That should help keep this thing on schedule."

He walked off, and Victor turned back to us. "Nice manners your friend Elton has," he said to me. Lloyd gave me a curious look, but Victor said, "Hey, Lloyd, since they're not shooting today, maybe we should get your flight done. It sounds like I'll have some high maintenance cargo later."

Lloyd nodded his agreement. "I'm anxious to see more of the area. It looks beautiful. Inspiring."

"It sure is," Victor said. He turned back to me. "Remember, you can take me up on that ride whenever you want."

And then he and Lloyd were walking away, talking about local canyons. I watch him go, not certain how to feel. He obviously enjoyed the Hollywood crowd, and they liked him well enough. But he paid particular attention to me. Maybe he did mean something by it. If I could just trust him—that he was more steady than a fluff of cloud, ready to dissolve if I really leaned on him. And how far might Victor lead me from home? My heart ached at the thought of leaving my parents and our little sanctuary behind, and I was terrified to take Victor at his word. If he was just teasing, just flirting, I would look like a fool if I fell for it. Like poor Jane with Johnny. Anyone on the outside could see Johnny wasn't serious. He was dating Thea, and even if that was just Hollywood politics, he would take those politics seriously. No, I wouldn't let myself be an idiot.

Speaking of Jane, I wondered if she was dressed yet.

I made my way back toward the ranch house and bunks where the Hollywood cast and crew were staying and poked my head in the girls' guest house.

"Has anyone seen Jane?" I asked.

A couple of girls shook their heads, but one piped up, "Oh, she stopped in here and did her make-up, but then a few minutes ago she said something about Johnny owing her something. I think she went toward the ranch house."

That brought a chorus of snickers and a few eye rolls from the girls. Apparently, everyone knew about her infatuation with Johnny. Poor Jane.

I trekked up to the ranch house. Other than my interview with the sheriff, I had stayed away from the main house since it was where the big actors were staying, along with the director.

"Jane?" I called in the entranceway, hoping Thea wasn't around.

"Up here!" she called.

I ran up the stairs to find Jane rooting around in one of the rooms. I paused in the doorway.

"Was this Johnny's room?"

"Yes," she said.

"You probably shouldn't touch anything. The sheriff will want to check it for clues."

She wrinkled her nose. "What kind of clues would he find? A note from someone saying they want to stab Johnny? Besides, he told me he had a present for me. He owes me that, at least."

I tried to frame an argument that she would understand. She yanked open a closet door.

She screamed, backing away.

I hurried forward just in time to see a skull roll out of Johnny's closet.

CHAPTER TEN

The skull was just bone. Mostly just bone. Very clearly human, though. It stared at me, its jaw open in a scream. I stared back as Jane shrieked and shrieked.

Voices and footsteps sounded from the stairs, and I finally pulled myself together and grabbed Jane, giving her a gentle shake.

She stopped screaming, but she still trembled, and her eyes had the glassy look of someone about to pass out. I wanted to tell her that bodies could look much, much worse, but it wouldn't have been helpful.

Instead, I led her back to the hallway, though she couldn't stop staring at the skull on the floor.

"What's all that racket?" Thea asked. Her eyes narrowed at Jane, and she waved her cigarette in the make-up girl's direction. "What were you doing in Johnny's room?"

I took a deep breath. "Miss Dove, please have someone call the sheriff."

"What do I look like, your—" She glanced into the room and saw it.

To give her credit, she didn't faint this time, just went a little pale. "Is that real?"

I hadn't considered that. When she wasn't hamming it up for the camera, Thea was surprisingly level-headed. The skull looked real, but what if it was a movie prop? That seemed a little more likely for someone to keep in a closet than an actual corpse.

"I don't know," I admitted. "But we need to have the sheriff look at it anyway."

Elton, who had come up behind us, said, "He's still here. I'll go get him."

He ran down the stairs. I stood, holding Jane and bracing myself to meet Sheriff Moore, all while breathing in the pungent stink of Thea's cigarette. The sheriff was not going to like finding me here. He would think I had been snooping. Jane might be able to vouch for me, but given her state of shock, she might not be much help.

Sheriff Moore was there within a few minutes. He glared at all of us and pushed past into the room.

"Is it real?" Jane asked breathlessly. "Is it real? Is it real?"

He examined it and gave a huff. "Looks real enough to me."

Jane took a breath like she was going to scream again, but I gave her another gentle shake.

"It touched me," she said, a sob catching in her throat.

Thea snorted. "You're lucky anyone would."

Jane's sob turned into a wail, and she lunged for Thea. Thea was ready with a firm slap. I grabbed Jane before she clawed the actress's eyes out. Which she seemed prepared to do.

"Johnny never cared about you!" Jane screamed. "He loved me!"

Thea gave a sharp-toothed feline smile. "Johnny loved Johnny. The rest was just a game. This is all a game."

"Someone is dead," I said. "Two someones."

Thea flicked her cigarette. "Then they didn't win, did they?"

Jane sank to the floor, bawling. I sat next to her. She still glared at Thea through bright, teary eyes.

Sheriff Moore watched with eyebrows raised. "Interesting. Now, why were you three in a dead man's room?"

"I wasn't," Thea said with a smirk. "At least not today."

Jane snarled and looked to the sheriff. "He promised me a present. He owed me a present!"

Sheriff Moore looked to me.

"Jane was looking for a present Johnny had promised her. I followed her to the house just in time to see..." I motioned to the skull watching us from the woven Navajo rug.

"You may have disturbed vital clues," Sheriff Moore snapped. "This is clearly about more than a grudge against an abrasive actor."

Thea raised an eyebrow, the smoke from her cigarette creating a hazy frame around her face. "Does this mean that Johnny murdered someone? I didn't know he had the guts."

The sheriff glared at her. "I don't know yet. I'll need a doctor to look at the remains and see what they mean. Until then, no one is to go into this room!"

I nodded my agreement and helped Jane off the floor. Her sniffling had slowed considerably. She just looked sullen now. Had some of her hysterics been a show? Maybe she really had caught Johnny's eye as a good actress.

We went outside to find a crowd gathered, Barry among them. He pushed his way forward to me.

"What happened in there? What's all the fuss?"

I debated how much to tell him, knowing anything I said would end up in the paper, but Jane made the decision for me.

"Bones!" she cried. "We found bones in Johnny's closet! He was a murderer!"

An excited babble burst out among the crowd. I winced. There was no taking that back now, but at least I could give Barry more accurate details for the paper.

"There are bones," I told him. "Or at least a human skull. Hidden in his closet. We don't know anything about it yet, including who it belonged to or why Johnny had it. Sheriff Moore is investigating."

Barry's eyes gleamed in triumph. There would be a special edition of the paper, and everyone would buy it for sure. I already knew what the headline would be: *Murdered actor had real skeleton in closet.*

I wondered what Victor would say about that—about all of this—but he'd flown off with Lloyd and missed all the excitement.

Only then did I realize I'd had my camera with me the

whole time, but I'd never even thought of snapping a photo. I wasn't turning into a crack journalist after all. Here I'd just given Barry an article about trying to remember the positive that each person contributes to the world, and now Johnny was going to be memorialized as the murdered Hollywood star who kept a skull in his closet. He was beyond my help in more ways than one.

CHAPTER ELEVEN

The kitchen tent became the epicenter of the gossip pandemic on the set. Everyone wanted some comfort, whether coffee, fried potatoes, or too-dry chocolate cake. While they ate, they told me and each other everything. None of which, I quickly realized, was reliable.

"Johnny hung around some shady characters in Los Angeles."

"Maybe he was a communist."

"It was the cocaine."

"I heard he spied for the Germans in the war."

"He always wanted to play Hamlet. I guess he took it too far."

Ginny picked her way through the crowd to stand beside me while I placed out cups of coffee and bottles of soda.

"It must have been traumatic to see the... the skull," she whispered. "Or did the war prepare you for this kind of thing?"

I shook my head. "On the battlefield, you expect to see horrible things. You don't expect to see them here at home."

"I'm sorry you had to witness it. I'm glad I wasn't there!"

Victor strolled in and grabbed a soda. He took a long draw from the bottle and shook his head. "Oh, Doll, I'm gone for a few hours, and you get yourself into trouble."

"This was not my doing," I insisted.

Lloyd, who looked wide-eyed and more disheveled than usual, said, "What actually happened in there? The rumors are outrageous."

"The truth is pretty outrageous," I said. "One of the girls went looking for something in Johnny's room, and she found a skull in his closet."

Victor took another swig. "That's pretty weird. Just the skull?"

"She didn't look any farther. And, no, I didn't, either. I called for the sheriff right away."

"It was just bone, then?" Lloyd asked. "Not, well…"

"Mostly just bone," I said quickly.

"I wonder what else they're going to find in his room," Victor said. "Sounds like the makings of another movie, eh, Lloyd? The flashy movie star who kills people on the side."

He smiled faintly. "Truth is stranger than fiction. It will be good publicity for the movie, though."

"Will it?" I asked. "I would think everyone would be horrified."

"Exactly. And they'll want to come see the last movie starring the notorious killer Johnny Fletch. Fritz has us writers scribbling Johnny out of the script, but he's planning on keeping all of the footage of Johnny, even his last scene."

"That's ghastly!" I said.

"That's show business." Lloyd wrinkled his nose. "They'll follow the money wherever it leads. It's the same reason they don't listen when I tell them what they're doing isn't accurate. It's all about what looks good on screen. What audiences will pay for."

I shook my head.

Rosie came up to the counter with Mel in tow. "Is it true? Were you really there?"

I gave her a brief run-down of what had happened.

Rosie whistled. "Wait until Javi hears. He'll be jealous."

"Isn't he around?" I asked.

"No, he ran off somewhere again after the sheriff questioned him."

I scowled. It was almost like Javi was hiding something. There was no way Javi had killed Johnny. The actor had been rude to him, but he'd been rude to everyone, and Javi wasn't violent like that. Maybe he just didn't like being questioned.

"Don't worry," Rosie whispered. "I'm sure he's not under suspicion. Not any more than the rest of us."

"The sheriff questioned you, too?"

Rosie nodded. "I wasn't on the set at the time. I was off having my make-up fixed."

"Well, that gives you an alibi. And Jane, too, I suppose."

Rosie's forehead wrinkled. "Actually, it wasn't Jane who did my make-up. It was the other girl. Mary Lou, I think? Jane must have been working on someone else."

I nodded. I hoped she was. Her obsession with Johnny didn't look good for her, though. Ginny was in the clear, at least. She had been on stage the whole time. And I had been next to Fritz and Willis the cameraman, so we were safe. But Thea and Elton had both been right there when Johnny died. Thea had been arguing with Elton about something—something she threatened to tell the sheriff about. Was it something they saw or heard that day?

And then there was everyone else working on the set. So far, everyone claimed they hadn't seen anything, but somebody must have. Maybe someone knew whatever secret the skull signified. Maybe more than one someone. How could Thea not know that her beau kept a skull in his closet?

Apparently, that question was on Sheriff Moore's mind, too, because Thea swept in a little later, her face a mask of outrage.

"That sheriff simply will not leave me alone!" she announced to everyone in general. "He thinks I must have known what Johnny was doing with human bones in his room." She shuddered. "So gauche! As if I would have anything to do with that. At any rate, Johnny kept his own secrets."

"Well-played," Victor mumbled.

I agreed. She was making a show out of this. Was it all part of the game she thought herself to be playing? Or had she simply forgotten how to stop being on stage all the time?

"It was bones then?" Lloyd asked. "Not just a skull?"

Thea shuddered. "They pulled out an entire human skeleton!"

All attention turned to Thea at that. Thea's eyes glittered in satisfaction. Her gaze fell on Jane, whose face was puffy from crying. Thea laughed bitterly.

"And you! Taking advantage of Johnny's death to tell everyone he loved you!"

"He did!" Jane shouted. "He was going to marry me and make me a star. We were meant for each other."

"You're delusional! I saw your love letters to him. We laughed at them together."

Jane stood, her face whiter than any stage make up. "That's a lie! I could kill you for it!"

The room went very, very quiet, everyone staring. Thea smirked a little. Wow. This just kept getting worse.

"Maybe," Thea breathed, "you killed Johnny when you realized he would never want you."

Jane shrieked and stormed out of the kitchen.

Victor and I exchanged worried looks. I started to go after her, but Victor caught my arm.

"All things considered, maybe you should give her time to cool off."

I didn't think Jane was going to murder me—I was pretty doubtful that she would have murdered Johnny—but I did see the wisdom in his advice.

Elton walked through a short time later. He gave Thea a cold look and stopped to flirt with Ginny.

"You know what I like about you?" he asked her. "You're still innocent. None of these jaded Hollywood lady airs about you."

Ginny raised an eyebrow. "But if I go to Hollywood, will it ruin me?"

"Hollywood has been the downfall of many a bright-eyed lady. But I think you have your head on better than a lot of those dames."

Ginny smiled and raised her soda bottle to him.

I felt ill. Maybe Ginny could avoid being corrupted by Hollywood. I wanted her to be happy. She seemed to like life on her homestead, being independent and in charge. But Hollywood might give her that as well.

At least she didn't take Elton's flirting seriously. I had spotted her catching up with Sam while she wasn't on camera, and the two of them had been cheerful. Given Sam's unrequited feelings for Ginny—and his dislike of Hollywood—he probably wouldn't look so happy if she'd announced she was leaving her homestead for California. Or maybe he wanted to go to California, too.

To distract myself from my worries, I took my camera to Willis when we both had a break.

"If you're willing, I'd love to get this film developed." I offered him the camera.

He smiled. "I'm happy to help a fellow film aficionado. You have anything good on this roll?"

I shrugged one shoulder. "Maybe. Lots of pictures of the crew, anyway."

"I'll let you know how they turn out," he said. "I should be able to work on them tonight."

"Thank you!"

I avoided Bo Young, who strutted around the set like he owned it, and made my way back to the food tent. Javi waited at the counter, his eyes wide.

"Did they really find a body in Johnny's room?" he asked.

I tied my apron back on. "You would know if you'd been around."

"Ah, come on. I had things to do with some of the fellows. Won't you tell me?"

I met his pleading eyes. "Fine. They found human bones in his closet. The sheriff hasn't told us anything else."

"Wow, bones! Creepy. I guess Johnny was a weirdo after all."

"What do you mean?"

"Just stuff I've heard the fellows say. That Johnny was always sneaking around. He had shady friends."

The same kinds of rumors I'd been hearing all day. It didn't mean there was much to them, but it made me curious. I would have to ask Sheriff Moore if he knew about Johnny's past. And I would get my chance, because I was sure the sheriff had more questions for me as well.

CHAPTER TWELVE

Murdered Hollywood star hiding human remains. Barry's headline splashed across the front of the special edition of the *Kane County Report*. I thought he'd missed out on an opportunity to use the "skeleton in his closet" line, but I hadn't earned the opportunity to write headlines. I was still fumbling with my article about locals on the set, and nobody would care about that until the murder investigation was over.

"Can't get much more sensational than that," I told Ginny as we looked over the paper early the next morning.

"Well, it is a sensational case. I suppose it will do us some good, though." She sounded like Lloyd.

"The movie, you mean?" I tried not to sound resentful. I don't think I succeeded.

She bumped me with her elbow. "No, silly! Kanab. Kane County. This movie was already going to put us on the map, but now everyone will be talking about it, and about us."

I glanced at her sidelong. Was this really about Kanab, or was it about her sudden rise to Hollywood fame? Either way, she looked more excited than worried. Was I the only one who thought it was a bad thing that people were dying?

Victor caught me in the kitchen later, scrubbing at a pot with more aggression than necessary.

"Hey, Doll, why the long face?"

"Well, there's been a murder, and everyone seems to think it's a great thing. I know Johnny wasn't popular, but he still didn't deserve to be stabbed. Or, his killer should be brought to justice, at least."

"Whoa there. You'll get no argument from me."

I turned, expecting to find him mocking me, but he looked serious.

I sighed and rubbed my eyes. "What's wrong with everyone? Why do I feel like I'm the one who's crazy?"

Victor took my hand, gently, and held it. "You're not crazy. You've probably got a better perspective because you've seen enough death to take it seriously. Everyone else has their heads in the clouds."

His finger traced a gentle path on the back of my hand, sending a thrill through my core.

"Do you?" I asked, my voice a little raspy.

"Not in the same way as them, at least," he said with a smile. A smile that was definitely directed at me.

"You're a flirt," I said, my breath catching.

"Maybe sometimes. I told you before, I've never been good at talking to women. I'm shy, so I hide it behind, well—"

"Your handsome smile?"

"You do think it's handsome, then?" He grinned.

"You must know it is, the way you throw it around to get your way."

"It doesn't seem to be working on the thing I want the most, though."

"Which is?"

His eyes, intensely serious, fixed on mine, and he pulled me closer. I let him, my head in a swirl. His thumb brushed a warm line down my cheek, coming to rest near my lips. "I think you should know by now, Hortencia Mateo."

His accent was terrible, but I didn't mind.

"How can I trust that you're being serious?" I whispered.

"Maybe you just have to take that first step."

A step away. Away from my family and our refuge here. And if he let me fall, I would be all alone. I groaned and squeezed my eyes shut.

"I still owe you a ride in the plane," he said, his voice soft and serious. "Just let me know when you're ready."

I looked up, and he caught my gaze, then smiled and walked away, leaving my heart in pieces. I didn't know what I wanted. No, I did know: I wanted too many things that I couldn't have all at once.

I turned to get back to work and found Thea watching me with narrow eyes. What, because of Victor? She had every man in Hollywood dangling after her. Why did she need Victor, too?

Sheriff Moore interrupted before Thea could make a scene.

"Sister Mateo, time for us to talk," he said, using the honorific familiar from church.

"Sister?" Thea cackled. "Are you some kind of nun? Does that pilot know? I don't think celibacy is his thing."

No, and I wouldn't want it to be. My skin was still warm where Victor had touched it. My face burned, and I didn't respond, just followed Sheriff Moore.

He escorted me into the parlor of the house where he had his temporary office. I sat across from him and folded my hands so I couldn't fidget. I hadn't done anything wrong. I'd even tried to stay out of the case. But that didn't mean the sheriff didn't make me nervous.

"Tell me what happened when Jane found the skull," he said.

I related everything I could remember, and he listened attentively.

"Did she invite you to go with her?" he asked.

"No. I was looking for her. I was going to take her picture, and one of the other girls told me she'd gone up to the house to get something Johnny owed her."

"So, you weren't with her the whole time?"

"No, I found her in the room."

"Then she could have taken something out of the room. Or put something in it?"

I looked up, surprised, and met his eyes. He would have made an excellent card player. His expression gave nothing away.

I nodded. "Yes. Either one. She said she was looking for a present, and she seemed sincere, but I don't know her well enough to guess." I couldn't help bursting out, "You think she put the bones in his room? Why? Where would she get them?"

Sheriff Moore barked out a dry laugh. "Where would anyone get a bunch of dried up human bones? I can't find any witnesses that saw anyone carrying a skeleton around." He rubbed his eyes. "An actual skeleton in a closet. That's actors for you, I guess."

"So, it was the *entire* skeleton?" I asked cautiously. Just clarifying, not being too curious.

He grunted. "In fact, it was. It would have been helpful to keep that to ourselves, but your friend Barry already spilled the beans to the whole county."

"I really don't think Jane could have planted a skeleton in Johnny's room."

"What about taking anything out with her?"

Had he found something missing? If so, he wasn't going to tell me. I considered his question. "She could have hidden something in a pocket before I got there. Nothing very big, though. And she was still searching when I arrived."

"What else do you know about her?" When I hesitated, he added, "You were... useful on that case with the bootlegger. I'm not deputizing you or anything, but I'm mostly getting gossip and hearsay from everyone around here, and you have a level head. I'd like you to keep your eyes open and tell me if you notice anything strange."

I perked up at the compliment and thought about Jane. "She's very dramatic. She fancies Johnny was in love with her and was going to get her a role in a movie, but I doubt it. Thea Dove mentioned some love notes."

"We're going through everything in Johnny's room right now. I'll keep an eye out for those notes. Tell me about Miss Dove."

One by one, he grilled me about the other cast members. What I'd seen. What I thought of each of them. Dangerous Thea, charming Elton, frantic Fritz. I could tell he wasn't taking my word for gospel, but it was gratifying that he listened. I even mentioned the argument between Javi and Johnny, since I didn't want to be found out in a lie. Sheriff Moore seemed much more interested in the Hollywood troupe than anyone local.

"And Rick Yazzie?" he asked.

"Oh, well, Johnny was rude to him, too. He was rude to everyone."

"Was Yazzie on the set during the murder?"

"I'm... not sure. He's playing one of the bandits. I don't think he was there." But I wasn't sure why the Navajo actor would have anything to do with Johnny Fletch. Johnny had been rude to him, but Rick had seemed to shrug it off.

"And Victor Holbrook?" he asked with a grimace.

I raised an eyebrow. "He wasn't there."

"Did he have an issue with Johnny Fletch?"

"Not particularly. He arranged to take Johnny for a ride in his airplane shortly before the murder, but it never happened. I don't think he liked Johnny, but he didn't have much to do with him."

"Well, I've fixed that hole in the ceiling of the courthouse if I do have to take him in again."

I tried not to laugh, remembering how Victor had escaped last time the sheriff arrested him.

"Your friend Ginny is in the clear," he added. "She was on camera the whole time. I can't say I'm sorry that I won't have to question her," he admitted with the faintest glimmer of humor in his eyes. Was he actually joking with me? That was a change. "What about her ranch hand? Sam Ellis?"

I hesitated a moment, feeling like a traitor. "He was on the set earlier, but I didn't see him after we found Johnny." Why was the sheriff asking about Sam? Sam wouldn't like to see Ginny go to Hollywood, but I didn't think he would stab Johnny over it. If anything, he would be jealous of Elton flirting with Ginny. "Bo Young was there that day, too, but he disappeared about the time Johnny was killed," I added for good measure.

The sheriff raised an eyebrow at me. It was no secret my family didn't like Bo Young, but if the sheriff was going to question me about my friends, he could hear about my enemies, too.

One of the deputies came down the stairs, his eyes wide. "Sir! You need to see what else we found in Fletch's room."

He was holding a pot that looked an awful lot like the one Javi and I had found in the old cliff house, plus a necklace of turquoise beads. The polished stones glinted in the light, almost like it was winking at us—telling us that it had a secret, and if we were lucky, we might figure it out.

CHAPTER THIRTEEN

Sheriff Moore bounded up the stairs. He hadn't invited me to come—that went well beyond asking for my insights—but he hadn't forbidden me from peeking, either. I followed upstairs behind him and the deputy.

The deputy had pulled a long wooden crate out from under the bed, and he was carefully searching through its contents. I braced myself. Was it full of more skulls? Various other body parts?

The deputy lifted a pale grey clay pot decorated with dark, geometric patterns. It looked like Johnny had been collecting Navajo pottery. This pot looked older and less colorful than the examples I'd seen, though.

The next piece he pulled out was broken. And another had different patterns. Not like anything I'd seen in Navajo villages, but it was familiar. I'd seen similar sherds when hiking up by the cliffs. Sherds from ancient pots.

Then the deputy lifted a necklace made of finely carved bone beads. "Like the one we found with the body," he said.

Sheriff Moore grunted.

"He was collecting ancient artifacts," I said.

Sheriff Moore swiveled to face me, his eyes narrow, and I realized perhaps I had overstepped by coming upstairs. Was he going to arrest me for interfering? He leveled me with a warning gaze and didn't deign to give me any more details. At least he hadn't thrown me out of the house yet.

"Is it illegal to take artifacts?" I asked. A lot of locals collected potsherds they found on their land. Land which, I supposed when I thought about it, had once not been ours.

"It is if he took it from public land," the sheriff said.

Which I guessed he did, since he was doing this in secret. Kane County was mostly public land—canyons and mesas and desert rocks sculpted by wind and water, which weren't hospitable for human settlement. Though, the ancient people had managed.

"And it's definitely illegal to take a body from its resting place," his deputy added.

I stared. "You mean that body..."

"It's not modern," the deputy said, ignoring a warning look from the sheriff. "The doctor said it's been mummified."

"Johnny Fletch was a grave robber!" I shivered to think of the handsome actor digging up bodies from ancient desert graves in the middle of the night. And how wrong to disturb those who were at rest, who had come long before us. Miss Grace would have a lot to say about that issue.

"And it's important that no one knows," Sheriff Moore said pointedly. "The killer or killers may have gone after

Johnny because of his grave robbing, and we want them to give themselves away. We don't want them to know what we know."

"Of course." I saw the logic in that.

"Your buddy Barry cannot find out about this. Once it's in the papers, we've lost our advantage."

I felt a twinge of regret. If I could write about grave robbing, it would definitely make the paper—and Miss Grace —more popular. But I understood the reasons for it. I would wait to write about it after the sheriff had arrested the murderer.

Which was who?

Sheriff Moore was interested in Rick Yazzie. An Indian wouldn't like someone stealing ancient artifacts or disturbing their graves. The Navajo people didn't claim relationship to the ancient cliff dwellers, though. They had been enemies. Rick Yazzie seemed like a stretch for a culprit. For that matter, so would Sam. He was Paiute. It seemed just as likely that Johnny had been shot for something having to do with women as smuggling. I wanted to make that argument to the sheriff, but he cut off any chance.

"That will be all, Sister Mateo. Perhaps you could send Mr. Holbrook in to see me?"

"He wouldn't be involved in grave robbing!" I protested.

The sheriff gave me a warning look, and I bit my lip. I had thought Victor wouldn't be involved in bootlegging either, and I had been wrong about that.

I nodded and left the ranch house, my mind whirling. I had to warn Victor. No, I couldn't. I couldn't tell anyone what Sheriff Moore suspected. Not that I thought Victor was guilty, or that he would blab. But I had to be careful not to land myself in trouble with Sheriff Moore.

Victor looked hopefully when I walked up to him in the kitchen tent, and I felt like a wretch for sending him into the lion's den.

"The sheriff has some more questions for you," I said.

He rolled his eyes. "I thought he'd had enough of my pretty face for one lifetime. You know, he warned me that he'd fixed the courthouse ceiling."

I couldn't help laughing. "Yeah, he told me, too."

"Do you know what he wants?"

I shook my head, then found a loophole. "Probably something about Johnny's movements. When he hired you to take him flying, did he say anything about wanting to land anywhere?"

"What, out in the desert? No, and even if he had, I would have said no."

I nodded, remembering a very bumpy landing on a mesa. "Was he interested in any area in particular?"

"Hmm. Yeah, he said he wanted to see the canyons. He mentioned Glen Canyon, but the Jenny wouldn't make it there and back without refueling. Why? What's this about?"

I shrugged one shoulder. "I can't say, but I imagine you'll find out soon enough."

Victor's lips twisted into a rueful smile. "Ah, Hortencia, are you getting involved?"

"No! Not exactly, anyway."

He gave me a knowing smile and walked off to find the sheriff. I watched him go, my feelings all mixed up into a painful knot in my chest.

CHAPTER FOURTEEN

I wasn't getting involved. Still, I'd been given permission to "keep my eyes open." That meant I could do a little snooping of my own. I wasn't going to spy on anyone. Just be observant. I could pass on what I noticed to Sheriff Moore, and also write about it later if it would make a good Miss Grace column.

My job in the kitchen was the perfect place for observing. Thea and Elton, for instance, pretended to be at odds with each other, but I noticed how they watched each other. How they whispered together, often angrily, when no one but the "help" was watching. They knew something they weren't sharing. Was it about grave robbing? It was hard to imagine that Thea didn't know what her beau was doing. Maybe Elton was blackmailing her.

Victor came whistling back into the kitchen tent after his visit with the sheriff. If he knew or guessed what Johnny had been up to, he gave no sign of it. He laughed and flirted as though everything were fine. Maybe for him, it was. He had nothing to worry about and nothing to hide.

Javi acted like he had everything to hide. He ducked through the food tent without meeting my eyes. He didn't get a ride home with Rosie and me, either, and, though I heard his bedroom door close late at night, I didn't see him doing his normal chores in the morning. My stomach clenched.

"What kind of trouble is he in?" I whispered to the clucking chickens as I tossed their dried corn and peas into the yard.

The birds made a mad scramble for the feed, scratching the red dirt and pecking each other for their favorite scattering of corn, though there was plenty to go around.

I stared off at the mesas to the north. Johnny had been stealing artifacts, and Javi knew where some were. I hated to think my brother might have sold the items in the cliff house to anyone from Hollywood, but he might have thought he was helping us. He wouldn't have killed Johnny. I couldn't imagine him doing it. But maybe he knew who did. Maybe he was in trouble. I had to help him, but I couldn't force him to confide in me. Of course, I didn't expect a teenaged boy to tell his older sister everything, but our family had always been close, and now it was falling apart.

The best I could do was to help the sheriff find who did kill Johnny. If that person was threatening or blackmailing Javi, arresting him or her would save my brother. I brushed my hands off on my skirt, shooed the chickens away, and cranked up the Model T to head over to the set.

Jane caught my attention in the food tent that morning.

She still wandered around looking weepy and daydreamy. What was going on in her mind? Was she still fixated on Johnny? Or was it an act?

Something glinted around her neck when she leaned down to pick up her plate of fried potatoes and scrambled eggs. She wore a turquoise necklace much like the one the deputy had pulled from that wooden crate. I stared at it, transfixed.

"Oh, do you like it?" she asked, sniffling and pulling the necklace free from her blouse. "Johnny got it for me."

Thea heard that, and she turned around to glare at Jane. If looks could kill, we'd have another murder on our hands.

"Mr. Fletch gave that to you?" I asked as casually as I could. "I wonder where he got it. It looks like Navajo jewelry."

Jane shrugged. "A girl doesn't ask those kinds of questions. I just appreciated knowing that he would give me something so precious." She shot a look at Thea.

As the two women glared at each other, I noticed who else looked positively sick about the whole conversation: Rick Yazzie. He stared at the necklace like he'd seen a ghost. Maybe he did know something about it.

It was Lloyd who broke the tension.

"What a lovely piece of jewelry," he said, taking Jane gently by the arm and guiding her to a seat. "I think Miss Mateo is mostly right. It is American Indian, but not Navajo. It looks much older than that."

"Oh, really?" Jane said, fixing her attention on Lloyd. "It is really valuable, then?"

"It's hard to say, but I imagine so," Lloyd said.

Jane stared at the jewelry with renewed fascination, a greedy glint in her eye. So, her sentimentality over Johnny had a financial side. Did Johnny really give the necklace to her, or had she taken it from his room? And was she really ignorant of the necklace's value and provenance, or had she been involved with Johnny's schemes? Someone had to know what he was doing, especially if he was selling the stuff.

Ginny sidled up to me. "I thought you ought to know," she whispered. "The deputy has taken Javi in for questioning. It looks pretty serious."

"Why?" I asked, too startled to keep my voice low.

"He's been spending a lot of time with Rick Yazzie, sneaking around. I don't know if they're looking for speakeasies or what, but Sheriff Moore is suspicious of Yazzie for some reason, so he's looking at Javi, too. I heard him say something about a local connection."

"That's ridiculous," I said. "The sheriff is grasping at straws."

But Ginny didn't know about the grave robbing. Rick Yazzie couldn't have been involved. He wasn't local. Not like Javi. Of course, most of us locals knew where we could find scattered potsherds and ruins from the people who lived and farmed here before us. Johnny probably did have someone local who told him where to find the ruins, but it could have been anyone. The Parry brothers could have let something slip when they talked up Kane County. Even Victor might have said something on one of his tours, though he didn't know the area as well. But just because they had tipped Johnny off to his grave robbing scheme didn't mean they were involved in his murder. Sheriff Moore had to arrest someone, but I needed to be sure it was the right person.

That settled it. Eavesdropping was not enough. I was going to have to investigate on my own. I could go places the sheriff couldn't without raising suspicion.

A warning voice reminded me that someone had stabbed Johnny, maybe over this same secret. I had to be careful. But I didn't want to see anyone innocent punished for Johnny's death—and especially not Javi.

CHAPTER FIFTEEN

I was determined to be systematic in my investigation, so I brought a pad of paper and a pencil and kept them in my apron pocket for notes. I jotted down the basic information I knew and the name of each of my suspects. Thea. Elton. Jane. Bo Young. Then I considered each of them.

Thea Dove. I underlined her name. She was hiding something. I needed to find out what.

Thea was surprisingly savvy, though. Maybe she was used to avoiding crazed fans or persistent suitors, but when I tried casually following her around the set, she always managed to slip off and elude me. If I kept following her, she was going to start to be suspicious. I needed to enlist help. Thea had nothing to do with Ginny, so my friend couldn't help me. It would have to be Victor. It turned my stomach, but if I sent Victor to flirt with Thea, we might find out more.

"Victor," I whispered, pulling him aside.

His eyes lit with hope, and I felt like a complete cad—if a

woman could be a cad—for making him hope for something I couldn't promise.

"I need your help," I admitted.

"Absolutely, Doll. Name it."

"I want to find out what Thea knows about Johnny Fletch's death."

He raised an eyebrow. "You don't trust the sheriff to figure it out?"

"He's looking at Javi. I know he didn't kill Johnny."

"I agree. He's not the type." Victor's simple assurance of my brother's innocence soothed me. "You suspect Thea?" he asked.

"Maybe. She's hiding something—she and Elton—and she's crafty."

"That she is." There was a bit of admiration in Victor's voice, and I felt a flare of jealousy.

"She also could be a killer!"

"Don't worry; I still like you better." He grinned and tapped the end of my nose.

I flushed. "I'm glad I rate higher than a murderess."

"You rate higher than all of them. After all, you're the only girl around here trying to solve a murder. No one else keeps life exciting like you do."

I pursed my lips in a scowl. "I'm glad you like excitement, because this could be dangerous."

"Making nice with the killer movie star?"

"Well, not *too* nice," I said.

He laughed, his eyes dancing with merriment. "You are darling. Of course, I'll help."

"Perfect," I said.

"I am—pretty nearly." He grinned.

I rolled my eyes. "Here's the plan."

We waited until evening, after supper when everyone had time to themselves. Victor had never arranged Thea's ride—the one Elton had paid for to make peace—so it gave him an excuse to draw her out, maybe take her to the plane. He could try to get her to talk, and I would search her room.

"What will you say if anyone finds you there?" Victor asked.

I held up a bracelet with a piece of turquoise. "I'll say I was returning this."

"Is it hers?" Victor asked.

"No, it's mine. And it's modern, but it might look enough like one of Johnny's stolen artifacts to get a reaction out of her."

"She's going to be suspicious," Victor warned.

"Hopefully I won't get caught."

Victor nodded at that.

Thea was wandering around the set, trailed by a few admiring stunt men and locals, and complaining about how dull Utah was. A perfect opportunity for Victor to draw her away. I hurried over to the house with my bracelet in hand.

I hadn't counted on Sheriff Moore posting deputies to stand guard. It made sense, though, with a killer on the loose and Johnny's accomplice out there somewhere. Someone, in theory, thought that there were valuable things in Johnny's room.

I approached the deputy as casually as I could manage. I recognized him from church, and I saw a flash of acknowledgement in his eyes.

"Evening Brother Sellers," I said.

"Sister... Mateo. Can I help you with something?" he asked.

"I found this bracelet in the kitchen. I think it's Thea's. I was coming to ask her about it."

His forehead wrinkled. "I don't know if she's in yet."

"Oh. I can wait in the parlor. I don't want to leave it in case it's someone else's."

I could see him weighing it in his mind. He wasn't supposed to let people in, but he knew me. From church, even. I was a terrible, terrible person for using that to my advantage, but I needed to get in there.

Finally, he shrugged. "Sure, go on in. I'll tell her you're here when she gets back."

"Thank you," I said.

That was going to cause problems. I went inside and headed to the parlor for a few minutes in case the deputy checked on me. Pretty soon, I was convinced he'd more or less forgotten me, and I headed up the stairs. The house was eerily quiet. A step creaked under my foot, and I jumped, looking over my shoulder. The evening sun cast long shadows in the rooms below, but none of them moved. My heart thumping hard, I hurried up to the landing.

I passed the door to Johnny's room and squelched any desire to peek inside. I was leaving that to the sheriff. But he wouldn't have checked Thea's room. He wouldn't have a reason to.

Her room was at the end of the hall. The door opened easily. It was perfectly orderly, almost sterile. I looked through drawers and her closet, but there was nothing out of place. No money or artifacts. A few hidden bottles of liquor, but that didn't surprise me.

Something thumped against the window. I peeked out. Victor waved frantically from the ground below. Thea was coming.

I hurried out of the room. Voices came from the stairs. I wasn't supposed to be up here, and I didn't want anyone to know I'd been snooping. The only two doors available for me to hide in were not good choices: Elton's room or Johnny's. I could not hide in Elton's. He might even be in there.

I opened the door to Johnny's room and slipped inside, leaving the door open just a crack.

"I'm tired of pretending, my dear," Elton said.

"So am I, darling," Thea responded. There was a rustle of clothing like two lovers caught in an embrace.

This was not what I expected. I held my breath as they drew closer. More sounds. Like kissing. Even more awkward.

"Oh, bother Johnny for having to go and die!" Thea said. "He ruined everything."

"I was looking forward to stealing you away from him."

Thea laughed coldly. "His expression would have been priceless."

"Why can't we just forget him now?"

"Don't you see how it would look? Everyone thought I loved him. It would ruin my image if I moved on too soon. But this can still work. Instead of staging a terrible breakup where you rescue me from that brute, we'll show them that we're slowly falling in love. It will still make a wonderful story for the press."

"I don't like the slowly part."

"Nor do I, but we must always think of our image. It's the cost of our fame. Together, we will be *the* couple in Hollywood, commanding top dollar and basking in the adoration of our fans."

"I only want *your* adoration."

"And you won't get it if you ruin both of our careers."

"You are cruel." Elton didn't sound put out—more like enthralled.

"Yes. It's best for you to know that now."

"You wouldn't be cruel enough to deny me one more kiss?"

"No, I would not."

More kissing sounds. Not pleasant to listen to. Then some murmured words of endearment, and a door opened and closed across the hall. Elton. He and Thea were just playing games with everyone while they followed their own scripts. I was quite fed up with Hollywood. I listened for the door at the end of the hall—Thea's room. It creaked and clicked, and I peered out. The path was clear. I hurried into the hall, heading for the stairs.

A sound behind me made me jump. Thea was watching me with narrow, knowing eyes.

"Oh, yes," she said coolly. "That cop by the front door said someone was looking for me." She raised both eyebrows. "Thought I'd be in Johnny's room, did you?"

"Oh, no, I just didn't know where to look."

"Sure you didn't. What did you want from me?"

"I, uh, found this bracelet in the kitchen. I thought it might be yours."

I held it up. Her lips curled into a nasty smile. "Why, it is mine. How kind of you to return it."

She slinked forward, a sharp curl to her lips. She wrapped her fingers around mine where I held the bracelet. They were cold, her nails long and sharp against my skin. I hadn't expected her to claim it. But I couldn't object now or it would look very odd. I smiled weakly and relinquished the bracelet. Luckily, it hadn't been precious to me, but Thea was sending me a message: I should not play games with her. She would take what she wanted.

I straightened my shoulders, determined not to show my vexation, and strolled back outside. Victor's steps matched mine as I put the house behind me.

"Sorry I couldn't keep her longer," Victor whispered. "Did she catch you in her room?"

"No. She caught me in Johnny's."

His eyebrows rose, and I told him what had happened.

He whistled. "So, that's their secret, huh? They are pretty good actors. I wouldn't have taken them for being in love."

"I'm not sure they really are," I said. "I think everything they do is a show at this point."

"Better to be regular folks with a shot at love, isn't it?" Victor teased. When I didn't respond, he said. "What's eating at you, Miss Mateo?"

"I'm worried about Ginny. And Javi. They're both getting caught up in this Hollywood glamor, and I don't want them to end up like Thea and Elton. Or like Johnny."

Victor was silent for a moment, then he put an arm around me. "Come here, Tenny."

His use of my name sent a pleasant shock through me,

and when he drew me closer, I didn't object. It felt wonderful to relax into his arms. Safe. Like I never needed to move from there. Like he would take care of me.

"They both have good sense," Victor said, his breath warm on my ear. "Well, your friend Ginny does. And teenage boys survive a lot of scrapes."

"Until they don't," I whispered.

"Sometimes, you have to trust the people you care about to know what will be best for them. And you have to trust yourself, too."

"Who says I don't," I mumbled into his coat.

"I think you're hiding from your heart," he said.

I sighed. It was hard to argue, wrapped in his arms but afraid of what my feelings meant. I wished I could stay there and forget it all. But I couldn't. I pulled away.

"What I know now is that Thea and Elton probably didn't kill Johnny. I don't think they had a reason to." I couldn't tell him about the artifacts, but they didn't seem to factor into Thea's scheming.

"Still, you have some news. Is Miss Grace going to write this up?"

I groaned. "It would make for good story. Juicy. Everyone would want to read about it. But that's not what I want to do. Not what I want to write about."

He smiled. "I'm glad you stand by your principles. I picture you more as the Nelly Bly type anyway."

I grimaced. "Locked in an insane asylum?"

He laughed. "Only if you don't learn how to stop fretting about other people's worries."

"Well, I'm still in danger then. Nellie Bly was only faking it, anyway."

And speaking of faking, the next person I needed to look at was Jane. I had some sympathy for her, but I couldn't ignore that necklace she had. She thought she loved Johnny, and she might have done extreme things to gain his favor.

I said good night to Victor and drove the Model T home, looking forward to some peace and quiet, but it was not to be.

Papa was finishing a new sawhorse by kerosene light, and the hammering echoed through the house. Abuela was in a flutter, mumbling to herself and scolding everyone who crossed her path.

Javi bounced over to me. "Hey, Ten! Guess what? Everyone is coming to the set tomorrow."

"They are?" I asked, looking at Mother, Papa, and Abuela.

Mother looked unhappy, but Papa nodded. "It matters to Javi, so we will take the time to do it."

It was a sacrifice for the entire family to miss a day's work on the farm, and the murder on the set hadn't endeared Hollywood to any of them.

Papa went back to his hammering, and Abuela went back to her muttering. Mother picked up her needle and stabbed viciously at her mending.

This would be interesting.

CHAPTER SIXTEEN

My entire family packed into the Model T the next morning after chores. Mother looked grim, and Abuela muttered a prayer under her breath as though she expected to be murdered as soon as we reached the set. Papa drove, and Javi chattered about everything he was going to show our parents about Hollywood.

When we parked at the set, I was happy to let Javi lead them away. It would be easier to investigate when I was not also trying to show Papa and Abuela around and keeping Mother from snapping anyone's head off. There seemed to be an extra buzz around the set for such an early hour. I went into the kitchen.

"Did you hear?" one of the other girls said, pouncing before I even had my apron on.

"Hear what?" I asked cautiously.

"Johnny Fletch was a grave robber!"

My shock was genuine. "Where did you hear that?"

Sytha smiled and held up the newspaper. "Everybody knows."

Cold flushed over my skin.

I did not tell Barry. I did not. I had to reassure myself of that, because I had wanted to, and now he knew. But unless Sheriff Moore had told Barry for some reason, he was going to think I had blabbed, regardless of my innocence. Oh, this was not good.

"I'll be right back," I said, tossing the apron back on its hook and running out of the tent.

I didn't even make it to the sheriff's office before he found me, his face almost purple and a paper crumpled in his hand.

"I thought I made myself very clear!" he boomed.

"I didn't tell anyone!" I said. "Not my family, not Victor Holbrook, definitely not Barry. I swear it."

He didn't look convinced. "Then who did?"

"I... I don't know. Who else knew?"

"Just you and some of my deputies. Maybe whoever we asked about the bones." His face puckered in a frown. "That's too many people to keep things quiet. I have to keep a lock on things. I'd better not see you as much as look in Barry's direction, though."

He left me shaken. I could have told Barry. I could have written the story myself and made a name as something other than an advice columnist, but I had kept my mouth shut. And now Sheriff Moore suspected me.

Grinding my teeth, I headed back for the kitchen.

Victor jogged over to walk alongside me. I gave him a dark look.

"I guess you heard the news?" he asked, then studied my face. "Oh, you knew! I should have guessed Nellie Bly would have her fingers in it."

"I knew," I growled. "But I did not write about it. Or tell Barry. And now someone else has, and I'm the one in hot water with the sheriff."

"Ouch! No good deed goes unpunished."

"It certainly seems that way."

"Did you want to write the story yourself?"

"Well, perhaps. Make sure it was told honestly and fairly. I'm tired of gossip."

"You and me both, Sweetheart. What now? I'm in on the secret, so is there anything I can do to help?"

I paused and considered him. "Bored again?"

"Just looking for an excuse to spend more time with you."

I blew out a puff of breath. "We need to find out who knew that Johnny was a grave robber. I'm going to see if Barry will tell me who his source was. If grave robbing got Johnny killed, then whomever knows about it could be the culprit. Or in danger."

"And if it was a crime of passion instead?"

"I'm going to deal with Jane today. I think she needs to be handled delicately, though."

"She is a bit... intense." Victor said.

"That's putting it kindly. I like her most of the time, but when it comes to Johnny, she was out of touch with reality. I'm not sure she can even tell me anything truthfully."

"Good luck, Doll. I'll do my bit around the set."

I nodded and watched him go. He really did seem to be on my side. But if he was sincere—if I admitted what I felt for him—wouldn't that take me away from my family? They needed me, especially if Rosie left with Mel Young and Javi kept wandering. I shuffled along the worn path between sage and rabbit brush, red dust clinging to my boots. I couldn't deal with that question now. One problem at a time.

I found Jane in the kitchen tent, deep in discussion with Lloyd. She looked nervous, her wide-eyed gaze darting around the tables, but Lloyd was smiling and shaking his head.

Lloyd spotted me and gestured me over. "Help us settle something, Miss Mateo."

"Sure," I said, watching Jane closely.

"You believe in ghosts, don't you, Tenny?" Jane asked. She clutched something in her hands. The necklace from Johnny.

"I've been telling her there's nothing to be afraid of," Lloyd said. "That's a nice piece of antique jewelry. It should be respected for the history it represents, but it can't hurt anyone."

Jane leaned closer to me. "I think Johnny may have stolen this necklace from a grave. I'm sure I'll be haunted now."

I looked at Lloyd, who clearly expected me to tell her there were no ghosts. He also clearly didn't know Abuela, who saw ghosts in everything.

I cleared my throat. "You know, I was a nurse in the Great

War. I saw a lot of strange things over there. Some I couldn't explain. I do think events can leave a mark on places—and things. Perhaps you should give the necklace to the sheriff. Tell him everything about it to be sure your conscience is clear."

"The sheriff?" Jane clutched the necklace.

"He'll probably just lock it away somewhere," Lloyd grumbled.

"He's not a bad fellow," I said to them both. Then to Jane, "I'll go with you if you'd like."

I was going to get in trouble for not being in the kitchen, but I'd do extra dishes to make up for it.

"Oh, would you? Thank you, Tenny! You're such a pal."

"Sure. Let's go."

I took her by the elbow and guided her to Sheriff Moore's office before she could change her mind. I didn't know how much she was really frightened of ghosts, but at least in the moment, she might spill everything.

Sheriff Moore did not looked pleased to see me, but his expression turned keen when Jane followed me inside.

"Jane has something she'd like to get off her chest," I said.

The sheriff adopted a kindly expression. He wasn't such a bad actor himself. Though maybe he did feel some sympathy for Jane. Something in her doe-like expression encouraged that kind of response.

Jane held out the necklace. "I took this from Johnny's room. He promised he'd give me nice things, but he never did. I thought it was a present for Thea, and I wanted it to be mine." Those fawn-soft eyes turned hard and predatory. The doe had teeth. Maybe she was a fox instead.

Sheriff Moore reached out a hand for the necklace.

Jane hesitated for a moment. "If this was stolen, I don't want to be haunted. If I give it back, the ghosts will leave me alone, won't they?"

"I have no doubt they will," Sheriff Moore said. "As long as there's not anything else you're keeping from me? Did you know Johnny was stealing?"

Her eyes welled up. "No! No, and I would not have believed it. Not until I saw in the paper that he had been robbing graves." She shuddered. "He was not who I thought he was. Maybe nothing he said was real."

She looked sincerely crushed. A girl who had just learned the world is not so much magic as illusion. Nothing about her demeanor made me believe she would fly into a rage and murder someone. She was an aspiring actress, but I wasn't convinced she was that good.

"Thank you, Jane," Sheriff Moore said.

He gave me a look that showed he had nothing more to say to me. I guided Jane out of the house. She drew a shaky breath.

"Thank you, Tenny! I feel so much better now. As if Johnny had some kind of spell over me, and now I'm free of him." Her eyes brightened. "Maybe he was a... a warlock. Maybe that's where he got his charm."

"Maybe," I said.

So, that was the direction her fantasies would take now. At least it would keep her away from romantic visions of

Johnny and his ilk. And she and Thea probably wouldn't have reason to butt heads anymore. Especially since Jane showed no interest in Elton, and Thea didn't care about Johnny anyway. She was just territorial. Like a mountain lion.

I was left feeling that none of them had stabbed Johnny. They didn't have reason to. But whom did that leave?

CHAPTER SEVENTEEN

Once I made amends to my fellow cooks by doing extra dishes, I decided to make sure Mother hadn't become the next movie set murderer. Papa would usually remind her to keep her temper, but he would be distracted by the movie making, and Mother lived up to all the red-headed stereotypes.

It turned out to be Abuela I had to deal with first. Rosie must have gone to film a scene and left our grandmother unattended. The sound of angry Spanish drew me to the site of Abuela's battle with Hollywood.

She'd cornered a poor extra dressed as a caballero and poured angry Spanish over him like glaze on a ham. He listened, frozen in terror.

"Hortencia!" she called when she saw me. She went on in rapid-fire Spanish, as deadly as a machine gun. "This man is supposed to be Spanish! A hidalgo! Look at him! He does not carry himself with pride. He does not even speak Spanish!"

I gave the actor an apologetic look and said in English, 'Abuela, he's an actor. He's not really Spanish."

"That is obvious!" she snapped in English. She turned to the man. "If you wish to be a *good* actor, you must learn to be like a Spaniard. You carry yourself with pride. Even if you are poor, no man is your master. Back straight. Chin up." The man obeyed, and Abuela nodded her approval. "Better. You must practice until you believe it."

"Yes, ma'am," the man said, taking the opportunity to escape.

"Bah!" Abuela said. "Hollywood! Now, show me where they are filming this movie about a Spanish hero."

With great trepidation, I showed Abuela to the set. They were filming a fight scene. Victor had been roped into taking part, pretending to give as good as he got. On screen, movie fights had always looked real, but seeing them film, it was almost comically fake, with the actors reacting to punches that didn't land and musicians playing jazzy music in the background. Abuela watched with her arms folded.

"Your handsome pilot pretends very well," Abuela said loudly. In English.

It didn't disrupt the actors, but a few of the onlookers gave us curious glances. My face burned.

The fight continued. One man snuck up behind Victor with his sword drawn.

"Ai! Señor Holbrook! Watch behind you!" Abuela called.

Victor glanced up, and several of the other extras looked over his shoulder. The man with the sword froze, not sure how to react.

"Cut!" Fritz yelled.

He whirled on Abuela. "Don't interrupt the scene! Do you know how much film costs?"

Abuela shrugged. "I saved you. The fight was bad."

The director looked like he wanted to show Abuela what a real fight looked like, and to spare him the embarrassment of being flogged by a Spanish grandmother, I quickly hurried her away.

"Why did you stop me?" she asked. "I was helping."

"Perhaps, but I'm not sure he wanted to listen."

"There wasn't even any blood. You'd think none of these people had seen a battle."

Abuela had seen far too many, in Spain and in Mexico. For that matter, so had I. "Blood doesn't look nice on the screen, I suppose."

"Hollywood!" she spat.

As I guided her a safe distance from the set, I considered what she said about blood. I'd seen plenty of it in the trenches. The sick, coppery stench still haunted me. A stab wound didn't bleed much while the bayonet or dagger was in it, but once it was pulled out, there would be blood everywhere. Whoever stabbed Johnny must have gotten blood on themselves.

Elton's black costume could have hidden blood, but the costume girls would have noticed when they cleaned it. They would have noticed that much blood on any of the costumes, and they would have said something if one of the costumes went missing. The killer couldn't have been one of the actors —including Javi.

I wanted to tell the sheriff, but first, I needed to find a safe place for Abuela.

One of the director's assistants jogged up to me. He gave Abuela a cautious glance and said, "Have you seen Rick Yazzie? He's supposed to come in at the end of this scene."

I shook my head. "I'll help you look for him, though." I owed them something after interrupting the scene earlier.

I went back to the kitchens. Everyone passed through there at one time or another. Sytha stood behind the counter on coffee duty. She gave me a polite nod.

"Have you seen Rick Yazzie?" I asked.

"Have I ever! He was in here earlier looking fit to kill someone."

"What happened?"

"I don't know. He didn't say anything. You know how quiet he is. But he was fighting mad. And he was carrying the paper with that article about Johnny grave robbing. I suppose he wouldn't have liked that much."

"I'm sure he didn't. Thanks."

I didn't dare leave Abuela in the kitchen because she wouldn't like how it was run, so I dragged her along with me. Of course, Rick wouldn't like knowing that Johnny had been grave robbing, but Johnny was dead. So, who had Rick wanted to fight? Johnny's accomplice?

Javi spent a lot of time with Rick, so maybe he suspected where Rick was or what he knew. I just had to find where Javi had gone with my parents.

I found my parents watching as Jane applied Javi's make-up for his next scene. Papa looked a little put off to see his son's face slathered in greasepaint, but Mother fumed.

As Abuela and I approached, Mother shook her head and

stepped up to Jane. I braced myself for a lecture about men in cosmetics.

"That's wrong," Mother said. She grabbed the eyebrow paint. "If you have to put this stuff on my son's face, at least make him look the part."

Jane's face reddened, and she opened her mouth to protest, but a look from Mother quelled her. Then, Mother set about drawing dark, threatening eyebrows on Javi as he squirmed. Jane watched for a moment, then nodded her approval and went back to the greasepaint.

Abuela's eyes bulged, and she stormed over to Papa, complaining in Spanish about how they were making Javi look like a clown.

"Javi, have you seen Rick?" I asked. "He's missing his scene."

Javi's brown furrowed, and Mother tsked at him to be still.

"That's not like Rick," Javi said, careful not to move anything but his mouth. "He was angry this morning, though. About Johnny. I think he went to say something to the sheriff."

"Thanks!"

I left them and dashed off to find Sheriff Moore.

"Did Rick Yazzie come see you this morning?" I asked before he could hassle me for being there.

His eyebrows drew together. "No. We he supposed to?"

"He was agitated about the news of the grave robbing. Javi said he might have had something to tell you, and now no one can find him."

As soon as I said it, I realized how serious the problem was.

Sheriff Moore rose to his feet. "Yazzie didn't have an alibi for the time of the murder, and everyone knows he didn't like Johnny. This doesn't look good for him."

"You can't suspect him. He was in costume the day Johnny died, and someone would have noticed the blood if Rick did it."

Sheriff Moore shook his head. "I thought he might be a suspect, but if he had information for me, I'm more worried that he's in danger now."

CHAPTER EIGHTEEN

By the next day, it was clear that Rick Yazzie had vanished. The sheriff sent out search parties, and everyone who came through the kitchen tent was gossiping about him.

"I bet he killed Johnny."

"He's just sleeping off a hangover somewhere."

"He was angry about the newspaper. Maybe he was involved and headed for the hills now that everyone knows they were robbing graves."

I slapped pancakes on their plates with extra ferocity. Not that they noticed. None of them cared about Rick or that he might be in danger. The locals saw him as part of Hollywood, and the Hollywood crew saw him as just an extra. But someone must have seen or heard a clue about what happened to him—something solid—so I tried to dig.

Fritz fumed when I mentioned Rick. "We're not waiting

for him to come back. We have to rewrite all of his scenes now. The writers are working overtime."

Fritz stomped off with his breakfast, and Jane took his place at the serving table.

"Did Rick Yazzie have his make-up done yesterday?" I asked her.

"Yeah, he did. First thing in the morning."

"So, he was planning on being at his scene. Something must have happened to him after that."

She shrugged one shoulder and slathered butter on her pancake. "Some of the fellows went up to hike the canyon before it got hot. Maybe he went, too, and got lost." Her eyes widened. "Maybe there are vengeful spirits out there in the cliffs."

That was a fanciful stretch, but it would be worth asking if he had left the set with anyone.

Ginny watched Jane and shook her head. "If all this fuss is over Johnny robbing Indian graves, I'm glad Sam hasn't been around. He wouldn't have liked that either, and he already has a bone to pick with Hollywood."

I was glad, too. I didn't want to see Sam in trouble or in danger. He was going to be angry—and heartbroken—if he lost Ginny to Hollywood, though.

When Javi came through, I interrogated him about Rick's plans.

"He knew we were in that scene," Javi said. "He wouldn't have missed it. And now Sheriff Moore is asking a bunch of questions like he thinks Rick did something wrong."

"He just wants to find Rick. He could be in danger."

Javi's forehead wrinkled. "Why?"

I lowered my voice. "He might have known or guessed who else was working with Johnny. And if they killed Johnny, they wouldn't be afraid to kill Rick, either."

Javi paled. "Rick was no grave robber."

"I don't think he was."

Javi went on as though he hadn't heard. "People are saying that Rick was the one stealing the stuff and Johnny was his connection to sell it. But Rick wasn't even from Utah. Or Arizona. It's not like he knew the area. He was just mad that anyone would steal Indian artifacts. And from graves!"

"It is pretty awful," I agreed. "You've gotten to know him pretty well."

"I have," Javi said defensively.

"If there's anything you can tell us about what he was doing, it might help us find him."

Javi hesitated, his lips twisted in a scowl.

"It's not worth keeping a secret if it might get Rick killed."

Javi rolled his eyes. "The only reason it was secret was because of you and Mother!"

Cold prickled over my skin, and my stomach tightened. "What is it?"

"You hate my music. You don't want me to play. Well, Rick is great on the guitar, too. We were trying to put a group together. We have this great sound: jazz, but with Mexican and Indian vibes."

"Oh." The tension drained from me, and my fingers relaxed on the spatula. "That's where you've been all this time? Practicing with Rick?"

"And a few other fellows."

"Is Rick trying to convince you to go to Hollywood?"

"No," Javi said with a snort. "We were just having fun. But I want to try to find some other guys around here to start a band with. Maybe we could travel around Utah and play. Salt Lake City and Ogden have great music venues."

I stared off into the distance. I'd rather have my brother in Ogden than Hollywood. But he should have been able to tell me all this before. Not sneak around just to play jazz with some friends. Mother and I had been trying to keep him so close that he had to wriggle away just to get some breathing room.

"I'm sorry I was hard on you," I said.

He shrugged. "Honestly, I'm more worried about Mother. I think Papa understands, but Mother never will."

"She will with time. It's just that after leaving Colonia Juarez. I think she hoped this would be permanent."

"It can't be! I'm not a farmer. There's nothing wrong with it, but it's not for me. I don't feel close to the land like you do. I feel like whatever I'm looking for, it's out there somewhere."

"What could be out there that's not right here?" I asked.

"You went to France!"

"And it was terrible."

"Just because you didn't find what you wanted, doesn't mean I won't. I don't even know *what* you want except to hide here all your life!"

Javi pushed off and stormed out of the kitchen tent.

I watched him go, my shoulders sagging. Was I hiding? Maybe. Trying to keep away from the ghosts of all the fighting and dying I'd seen. But they could find me here, too.

I was simply bone-deep tired of watching things crumble apart time after time. I wanted something I could hold onto. But it was like trying to hold sand in the wind.

I helped with the dishes and made a few notes on my pad of paper. I had to find out about this hike up the canyon. Even if Rick didn't go, maybe someone remembered seeing him around that time.

I hung up my apron and stepped out into the heat of the late morning sun. The bright light made my eyes water, and I sneezed.

"Who was that?" Bo Young asked.

I groaned inwardly. I'd been lucky enough to avoid him lately—especially yesterday while my family was on the set —and I didn't want to break my streak now.

"Could be anybody," said the kitchen manager. "Why does it matter? We're haggling over the price of bacon, not sharing state secrets."

"I don't want anyone trying to under sell me," Bo grumbled.

I shook my head and snuck off in the other direction to see what I could learn about Rick Yazzie's expedition.

As I asked around, though, no one seemed to know about the trip up the canyon. I found Jane and tried to pin her down about any details, but she just shrugged.

"I overheard someone talking about it yesterday. I don't really remember who. It just seemed like it was some of the fellows. Extras and stagehands."

I started to worry that Jane was lying, or that she hallucinated things, but Mary Lou, the other make-up girl, tilted her head.

"I remember that, too."

"Was Rick Yazzie with them?" I asked.

"I don't remember," Mary Lou said. "I don't even know if they actually went. Sorry."

A dead end.

I trudged back toward the kitchen tent. A warm breeze from the canyon brushed through my hair, and it brought an idea. Victor might know about any sight-seeing the Hollywood folks hoped to do. I had a few minutes before it was time to start lunch. I hurried toward the field where he kept his plane.

It was Victor who found me, his face unusually serious.

"What happened?" I asked.

"They found Rick Yazzie."

My hand went to my mouth. "Is he..."

"He's alive, but only barely."

"What happened? An accident?" But I knew it wasn't.

"Someone looking for lost cattle came across him in the cliffs up the canyon. He'd been beaten pretty badly."

"Left for dead."

"Looks that way."

"He knew something. He figured out who Johnny was working with."

"Probably," Victor said. He put an arm around me, and I leaned into it. "You all right?"

"Not really."

Sheriff Moore marched over to us. "Well, I hope you're satisfied. That information you leaked to Barry almost got Rick Yazzie killed. Maybe did get him killed—we don't know yet. And he may be our only lead about who was working with Johnny."

"Hey," Victor said. "She's not the one who talked to Barry. Clean up your own house before you start slinging mud around."

The sheriff snorted and stormed off. I trembled and tightened my grip on Victor, doing my best not to sob on him.

"Thank you," I whispered into his shirt.

"Anytime, Doll. I don't get to play the white knight very often."

I sighed and straightened, blinking away hot tears. "This is all because of Hollywood. I wish none of this circus had come here!"

"None of it?" Victor said, his voice light, but his expression a little hurt.

I sighed. "I don't mind you coming to visit. But not all of these people, with their secrets and their problems."

"I thought this was helping Kane County."

"It's not! It's going to ruin it! Outsiders coming in and trampling everything to pieces."

"I had hoped there might be room for one more outsider," Victor said. "If he wanted to stay?"

I stared at him. Was he really thinking of moving to Kanab? My chest warmed at the thought, but it quickly turned cold again. It wouldn't just be Victor. If this movie wasn't a disaster, Hollywood would come again. Tourists. They would spoil everything. And if the movie was a disaster, everyone would stay away, and we would wither and die. No matter what happened, it was like trying to grasp handfuls of sand: the grains poured through my fingers, whisked away by the wind, and I didn't know what to hold onto.

"I'm scared," I whispered.

Victor pulled me close again. "I know, Tenny. I know."

And I wanted to hold onto him, the solid feel of his chest against my cheek, the scent of his aftershave, the gentle touch of his fingers stroking my hair. But another breeze from the canyon blew over us, reminding me that nothing was solid enough to hold forever.

CHAPTER NINETEEN

While we waited on news about Rick Yazzie, I took refuge in the kitchen. I couldn't help Rick Yazzie. Or Sheriff Moore. Or Barry. I didn't know what to say to Victor. I was lucky I could cook a bowl of soup. Maybe that was my future. While everyone else moved on, I was going to stay in Kanab to cook and wash—a never-ending stream of chores the only constant in my life.

Ginny found me drying the big pots while the other girls washed. Sweat plastered my hair to the back of my neck, and my skirt was coated in red dust. Ginny wore a lacy dress, and her make-up highlighted her large, brown eyes and determined mouth. She was made for going places.

She sat beside me, unconcerned about getting her costume dusty. "The cameraman, Willis, was looking for you. Something about your film?"

"Oh, he developed my pictures! I wonder how they turned out."

"He seemed excited to talk to you, so I would guess they're good." She smiled and bumped my shoulder with hers. "That pot can wait, and they're taking a break from filming soon. It looks like it might rain on us later."

I hesitated, not wanting to leave the other girls.

Sytha shooed at me with her dish cloth. "Oh, go ahead. We're almost done anyway."

I left the pot, my apron—and my self-pity—behind to follow Ginny. Maybe I had some hope of *National Geographic* after all.

We hurried over to the set where Elton and Thea were filming a romantic rendezvous. I ignored them and watched the other people working on the set: the musicians, the cameramen, the writers, the stunt men. Victor wasn't there. He was probably taking someone on a plane ride. But a lot of locals were working behind the scenes, laughing and chattering while Thea and Elton put on their performance. It cheered me to see familiar faces looking more hopeful.

"Are you going to miss this when it's gone?" Ginny asked.

"Honestly." I smiled ruefully. "Not really. You?"

She laughed. "I will, a little. But not much."

I gave her a sideways glance. "You're not..."

"Chasing the golden dream?" she asked, eyebrows raised. "No, it's fools' gold, and I know it. But, I have three actresses absolutely addicted to my angora. *I'm* not going to Hollywood, but my fashions are."

"You're staying on your homestead?" My heart lightened a little at the prospect. I wanted my friend to be happy, but if she could be happy here instead of in California, so much the better for me.

"You really thought I'd go anywhere else?" she asked with mock offense. "This is where I'm free. The movie was a bit of fun—a new entry for my scrapbook—but when it's done, I'll just turn to the next page."

The director motioned to Ginny.

"Oh, I'm on again!" she said. "It will be nice to not having anyone calling me but the cows and the chickens."

Ginny took her place on the set, leaving me to think about what she'd said about turning to the next page. I watched Willis. His huge camera took shot after shot, stringing them together until they made the motion picture. One image by itself didn't tell a story. They had to move for it all to come together.

I had been trying to hold still. Like the desert. But even the desert was constantly changing. Juniper trees put roots down deep and wide to survive for centuries, but the winds twisted the ancient trees into tortured forms. Canyons walls stood tall and proud, but wind and water carved them into strange, undulating shapes a few grains of sand at a time.

There was no holding still. Maybe the best I could hope for was deciding how I would let the wind shaped me.

The breeze picked up, bringing the distant scent of wet sage. The storm was on the mesas.

Fritz called cut, and Willis stepped away from his camera and spotted me.

"Miss Mateo! Come over to the camera. I have those pictures ready."

"Thank you. Did they... turn out all right?" I asked shyly.

He grinned. "Wait until you see."

Ginny was talking to one of the costumers, so I waved to her and trotted after Willis.

He shared work space with the other cameramen in a tent. A long string hung across one wall with my photos clothes-pinned to it.

One of the other cameramen smiled at me and nodded toward the pictures. "Good work there."

I grinned my thanks and hurried over to study the little black and white rectangles. A few of the portraits had turned out blurry, which was unfortunate, but the pictures of the desert were crisp and clear, capturing the light playing off old juniper trees and ripples of sand.

"Those shots of the canyon walls were especially nice," Willis said. He stopped and frowned, pointing to a blank spot on the string. "Where did they go?"

I stared at the empty string, trying to remember what pictures were missing. Javi's canyon. And the pictures of the cliff house. A chill settled in my stomach.

"Did someone take them?" I asked.

Willis huffed. "Looks that way. I suppose it's a compliment that someone liked your pictures well enough to take them. Hey, don't look like that. I still have the negatives. We can make another copy."

"Thank you, but I need to know who took them. Didn't you notice what they were?"

"Some Indian stuff?"

"Artifacts. The kinds grave robbers go after."

Willis whistled. "Okay. We'd better ask around." He hailed the other cameraman. "George, do you remember anyone coming in here to look at these pictures?"

"Uh." George scratched his nose and looked thoughtful. "Oh, yeah. One of the writers. Lloyd, I think. Said he was looking for inspiration."

"Is he still around?" Willis asked.

"I haven't seen him for a while," George said.

Worry buzzed in my ears. I hadn't seen Lloyd since breakfast. And he hadn't been on the set when Johnny was murdered. Lloyd loved history. Did he love it enough to steal it for himself? To kill for it?

CHAPTER TWENTY

I had trouble picturing Lloyd as a murderer, but if he had only wanted my pictures for inspiration, why take the photos of Javi's canyon? Those were the clue about how to find the cliff house.

"We need to find Lloyd," I said. Either he was a murderer, or the killer might hunt him down like he'd done to Rick Yazzie.

Willis nodded, seeming to understand the urgency, and we split up to look for the missing writer. Willis jogged around the set, calling Lloyd's name. I hesitated a moment, then ran to Sheriff Moore's office. I might be in his black book, but he needed to know about Lloyd.

I burst into the ranch house and found one of the deputies there.

"Where's the sheriff?" I gasped, trying to catch my breath.

"He went out to talk to the rancher who found Rick

Yazzie. Why?"

I huffed and stared out the window, wondering how long I dared wait. I could leave a message with the deputy, but someone on the set had been blabbing to Barry, and if it wasn't me, it was probably someone in the sheriff's office. I didn't want to smear Lloyd's name to the papers if he turned out to be innocent.

"Tell him I was looking for him, please," I said.

I headed back for the kitchen tent. I wasn't sure who around the set was untrustworthy, but I knew at least one person I could count on. Victor. The thought warmed me. Yes, he would help me make sense of this. I would leave a note for the sheriff and find Victor.

Most people had cleared off the set in anticipation of the coming rain, but a few girls were still hanging around the kitchen tent. I went to get my notepad out of my apron, which was hanging with the others in the back.

The notepad was gone. I checked the pocket again, then looked at the other aprons, but their pockets were empty as well. I stood holding my apron, my mind turning. All my notes were gone. I'd used initials instead of full names and written in shorthand, but it wouldn't be difficult to figure out who I was talking about.

I turned to the other kitchen girls. "Has anyone seen my notepad?"

A couple of them shook their heads, but Sytha looked guilty. I folded my arms.

"All right," she said, pulling it out from under the table and holding it up. "I've been reading it. It was interesting," she added defensively. "I don't know why you were keeping all that news a secret."

An idea struck me. "You were the one who told Barry."

She nodded sheepishly. "He came around asking if we knew anything. He's from the newspaper. Don't people have a right to hear what's happening under their noses?"

"Not when it interferes with catching a murderer," I snapped.

Sytha lowered her head. "I didn't see any harm in it."

I sighed. I shouldn't have left the notepad where people could find it. I was Barry's source after all.

"Whoever killed Johnny is still out there, and he's dangerous," I said, retrieving my notepad and scrawling a message to the sheriff. "I might have a clue that will help, and I need you to deliver this to Sheriff Moore so he knows."

Sytha nodded enthusiastically. "Okay, but where will you be?"

"I'm going to see if Victor—Mr. Holbrook—can help me find Lloyd."

Sytha took the note, a determined glint in her eye. "You can count on me."

And I believed that I could. I gave her a smile to show that any hard feelings were past. Then I headed out the back of the kitchen tent and toward the field where Victor parked his plane. He wouldn't want to fly in this weather, so he ought to be around.

A strong hand grabbed my shoulder, and another hand clapped my mouth shut before I could scream. Someone pulled me close—a man, tall and with a wide chest, who smelled like coffee and sweat. I struggled, tried to bite the hand over my mouth. A glass bottle pressed between the fingers, against my lips. I smelled the bitter stench of laudanum, and the liquid poured between my teeth. I tried to spit it out, but the man tilted the bottle, dumping it down my throat. It burned, and I gagged. Choking. I couldn't breath and howled in desperation against the hand holding my mouth shut.

The man shoved a dirty-tasting cloth in my mouth and tied a bag that stank of onions over my head. I tried to wriggle away, kicking out behind me, but the man shook me violently. My stomach heaved, and the world spun around me. The laudanum was taking effect, Soon, I wouldn't be able to fight at all.

I dropped down, hoping to roll away from my attacker and dislodge the bag. But when I hit the ground, my movements were sluggish and slow. No, no, no. I was losing. I tried to scooch away, but fell flat, my head spinning with black. It was worse—much worse—than being trapped in a small, dark place, when that small dark place was inside of me. I made another feeble attempt to shout for help, but only a mumbled grunt escaped the rag in my mouth. As the darkness won, I thought I heard laughter.

CHAPTER TWENTY-ONE

"Miss Mateo?" a gruff, male voice asked.

I awoke slowly, groggily. I was... in the desert? Lying on the hard sand, the sky cloudy and the air scented like rain and a hint of laudanum.

Memory rushed back, and I sat up. My head throbbed with pain in response. Someone had kidnapped me. And left me to die like Rick Yazzie?

A dusty Ford truck waited nearby. And Bo Young sat on his haunches, watching me with a superior sneer.

"You kidnapped me?" I gasped.

He guffawed. "Now why would I do that, Miss Mateo? I found one of those Hollywood fellers out here with you."

He gestured to the truck. I pushed to my feet, my head reeling, and stumbled to the bed of the truck. Lloyd slumped there, eyes closed and a bloody lump on his head. His skin was pale, but his chest rose shallowly. I looked back to Bo.

"I took care of him," Bo said, and he waved a finger. "Not

as a favor to you. I don't want strangers out here bothering my cattle."

"I suppose I have to thank you anyway." I leaned on the truck.

Bo swaggered up next to me and grabbed a burlap sack. "Thank me by telling me where these came from."

He pulled an ancient pot out of the sack.

My mouth went dry, and I licked my lips. "I don't know."

"Come on, Miss Mateo. That's what he brought you here for ain't it? I want to get rid of the thing. I don't want treasure hunters out here spooking my cattle. Show me where it goes, and then we'll take that feller back to the sheriff."

I glanced toward the cliff house, but something tickled my mind. Something was wrong. That was Bo's truck, and it was parked near Javi's narrow canyon. Bo knew where it was. Of course he did—he was a local, and he used this land for his cattle. But how would Lloyd have known about it? He couldn't have found it by himself. He might have flown over the canyons with Victor, but the world looked very different with your boots on the ground. A cold chill crept over my flesh, pricking all my senses to life.

Bo Young wouldn't care about returning an ancient pot. He thought everything on these lands belonged to him.

I gestured to Javi's dry wash. "It's down that way. But it doesn't matter if you put it back. Just take it with you or toss it back into the desert."

"Now, Miss Mateo, that doesn't sound like the right thing, and I know you want to do the right thing."

Cold sweat broke out over my skin. I was trapped like an

injured jackrabbit facing a coyote. Bo watched me with sharp, hungry eyes, and he would have a gun. It would be easy enough for him to say that Lloyd had shot me. Just like he had skirted any responsibility in the bootlegger murders. I had to play along. "Of course. Let's see if we can find the way."

I led him over to the dry wash. The narrow strip of darkness mocked me, and I glanced again at the clouds on the horizon. "It would be safer to wait until that storm passes."

"It's far away enough, and we might not have much time until Lloyd comes to. I don't want to shoot anyone unless I have to."

I looked at him quickly, saw the threatening gleam in his eye. He smiled. "You go down first."

I nodded, my throat dry and my head dizzy. I did not want to go down into that crevice, especially not with clouds on the horizon. But I wanted to be shot even less.

The walls of the little canyon closed around me as I wiggled my way down. I thought for a moment that the darkness would take me again when my boots reached the sand, but I took slow breaths and squeezed down the canyon, wondering if I could outrun Bo. The waves and undulations in the canyon wall might make it harder for him to shoot me, but I still didn't feel stable enough to run very far. Bo was wider than me, though. Maybe he would get trapped by those tall, narrow walls.

He made his way down with a great deal of grunting and swearing. I scooted farther down the canyon, putting some space between us. The side canyon didn't feel as long this time, now that I knew it opened up. But as I neared the mouth of the canyon, my boots squelched in the sand. There was water in the wash. A storm upstream. We could not be caught there.

"The water's flowing!" I called. "We should head back!"

"Like hell!" Bo responded behind me. "Keep going!"

I leaned against the cool, water-sculpted walls, my pulse pounding in my ears. I didn't have much chance against Bo, but no one could withstand the force of a flash flood.

"Tenny?" came Victor's voice from somewhere above.

I heaved a great sigh of relief. "Victor!"

"Where are you?"

"Down in the little side canyon. Bo Young is here, too!"

"I've got the sheriff with me," Victor said.

Bo couldn't shoot me now, not with witnesses. I could hear him behind me, grunting as he struggled to climb through some of the narrow spots.

"I can't figure out how to get to you." Victor sounded almost frantic.

"I'll try to climb up."

I managed to find some hand- and footholds, pockmarks formed in the stone over the years, and climbed up to a narrow ledge, but the walls from there were sheer. I could see the sky through the crack in the earth above, but it was impossibly far above. Water sloshed around the bottom of the canyon.

"I'm trapped," I called.

"Hold on! The sheriff has a rope!"

After a few heartbeats, a rope smacked against the wall next to me. They had taken the time to tie knots in it. I climbed with trembling hands until Victor and the sheriff reached down and grabbed me under the shoulders to haul me into the open.

I lay on the sand, gasping in lungfuls of fresh air. Victor cradled me, and I clung to him.

"Bo!" Sheriff Moore called. "It's going to flood. Get out of there."

I glanced over and saw two of his deputies watching with their guns in hand.

I pushed myself up and peered down into the crevice.

Bo either didn't hear the sheriff or his pride couldn't bear to turn around. He sloshed through the calf-deep water, moving as fast as he could without letting the water sweep him off his feet. He was almost to the main wash.

The sheriff swore and motioned to his deputies. "Go downstream. Get ready to haul him out."

They jumped over the gash in the earth and ran to the tall, steep banks of the wash.

A sound came like a furious gust of wind. The water in the wash came faster, foaming with red bubbles.

Bo's head snapped upstream, in the direction of the flood. He tried to run, but the rushing water grabbed him, trapped him in its hungry current.

A mass of dark mud and fallen trees streamed down the wash like bubbling molasses. It almost looked slow enough for Bo to escape. He glanced over his shoulder and kept slogging forward, trying to reach the bank. The churning flood gained on him.

"Climb!" the sheriff called.

I didn't know if Bo heard, not over the rush of the flood.

He raised his arms. The water took him. For a moment, I could see his frightened face as he fought the current. Then, it battered him under, and he was gone.

The desert had never been his, and he knew it too late.

I winced and turned away, grateful for the comfort of Victor's embrace.

CHAPTER TWENTY-TWO

This time, I wrote the article. Not as Miss Grace, but as Hortencia Mateo. I told the facts as far as we knew them. About how Bo and Johnny had gotten into business together smuggling local artifacts. How, according to his account, Lloyd had helped Johnny evaluate the objects until they crossed the line into grave robbing. I had heard them arguing, Johnny threatening to blackmail Lloyd. From there, Lloyd claimed he had confronted Johnny but hadn't meant to kill him. That will be up to the jury to decide. There are some things we can never know for certain.

Rick Yazzie would recover from his injuries, though Bo had left him to die out there in the desert when Rick became suspicious and questioned him. Rick was considering leaving Hollywood to return to New Mexico. He wanted to make music instead of movies, and the desert inspired him. Maybe I'd write a story about him someday, too.

Bo's funeral service was held at the Pahreah church

building. My family attended to support Mel. His emotions hid behind his tin mask. With his father gone, he was considering staying in Kane County. He and Rosie could run the ranch and watch over Mother and Papa, too. Ironically, Bo might get his wish to see the two ranches united some day, just not in the way he had expected. Mel and Rosie sat together in the front of the church.

Victor sat in the back with me. The crowd was thin, and most eyes were dry, but we still gave Bo a proper memorial service. He had been one of us.

After the service, when the Young family went to the Pahreah cemetery, the rest of us stayed behind. Victor escorted me out into the warm sun.

"Have you finished the article?" he asked me.

The one I was writing about protecting historical sites. I hoped *National Geographic* would be interested.

"Almost," I said. "I'd like you to read it when it's done."

Victor nodded. "You know, with a willing pilot at your disposal, you could travel to all kinds of interesting places to take pictures and research your articles."

My heart fluttered the the thought, and this time, I didn't shy from the feeling. "I suppose I could, couldn't I? But where would I find such a pilot? They're all so busy shooting movies in Hollywood. And he can't just be any pilot. He has to be brave, not completely goose-witted—"

"Quite intelligent, I would say!" Victor said with one of his grins.

"And handsome."

Victor exaggerated a wince. "Oh, well that eliminates almost all the pilots I know. In fact, it leaves only one."

I raised an eyebrow at him. "Well, you'll have to introduce me, then."

He laughed and took my hand, drawing me nearer. "I've been hoping to let you get to know him even better."

I smiled up at him. "I'm looking forward to it," I whispered.

He traced his fingers along my jaw and leaned in for a kiss. I pulled him closer and kissed him back.

He stopped with a sigh and rested his forehead against mine. "I knew you couldn't resist me, Doll."

"That's 'Sweetheart' to you."

He grinned. "You know, this works out pretty well for me, too. You can write articles about your dashing pilot husband. It will be good publicity of my air tours of the local sights."

"Oh, will it?" I asked. "You can't just assume I'm at your beck and call. That might take some negotiating."

"I think I can manage that," he said.

And he pulled me in and made a very compelling argument.

AUTHOR'S NOTE

Kane County and Little Hollywood

Kanab, Utah's history as Little Hollywood dates back to the 1920s. The first movie filmed there was Western star Tom Mix's *Deadwood Coach*, released in 1924. The Parry brothers were the driving force behind introducing Kane County to Hollywood. They ran a business giving tours of newly-established Zion National Park, and while selling the area to early tourists they also promoted it to Hollywood executives. One of the brothers, Chauncey Parry, had learned to fly in training for World War I and later flew his biplane over Zion and the Grand Canyon—supposedly the first person to fly into the canyon—so Victor might have had some competition for his tourism-by-air business.

Kane County residents often found work on the local movie sets (I have my great-grandfather's stage pass from his time working behind the scenes for "Little Hollywood"). With farming experiencing an early depression following World War I, the extra work was a welcome addition for many families.

Kanab was one of the most remote towns in the continental US in the early 1900s. Electricity didn't reach it until the late 1920s. That was good for providing undeveloped landscapes for movies, but it also meant that residents of Kanab didn't have a theater to watch the movies they helped create until 1934 (the earliest I've been able to find). Before that time, they had to make the long trip to Panguitch or St. George to see motion pictures. Both of those towns had movie theaters by 1909 and 1911.

Film make-up was an emerging art form in the 1920s, evolving from earlier stage make-up to help actors look more natural on film. Many of the make-up specialists during this time were men like Max Factor, who founded the cosmetics company named after him, but I have found pictures of women doing hair and make-up and used them as a basis for Jane and Mary Lou.

Though white actors sometimes used make-up to play the role of Natives in early movies, many Native people did participate in movie making—sometimes portraying their own culture, but more often cast in stereotypical roles.

Zorro made his first print appearance in the 1919 book *The Curse of Capistrano* by Johnston McCulley, which was a hit at the time and is still fun to read today. Hollywood was quick to pick it up and released *The Mark of Zorro* in 1920, starring Douglas Fairbanks. Elton Fairchild is a nod to this first movie Zorro.

Other historical tidbits

The Vest Pocket Kodak was an innovative camera that helped bring photography to the masses. It had a telescoping lens that collapsed flat so the camera could fit in a pocket, and a little window where the photographer could write a note on the negative about the picture. Some soldiers took them overseas to the Western Front. The cameras were also used by everyone from explorers to families. Its photographs were black and white; there were a few experimental methods for developing color pictures, but they would not be common for several decades.

Southern Utah has the most slot canyons of any area in the world. These narrow canyons are beautiful and fun to explore, but never hike in them when clouds are anywhere in the area—flash floods in slot canyons are deadly. It is also home to some of the cliff houses typical of the Anasazi or Ancestral Puebloan culture of the Four Corners region. Many are easy to view on hikes, but they should never be disturbed since they represent fragile clues to the past that we are still trying to understand.

For further reading

The Parade's Gone By... by Kevin Brownlow is a history of early Hollywood, interesting for its details about on-screen and behind-the-scenes work on silent pictures.

When Hollywood Came to Town: A History of Moviemaking in Utah by James V. D'Arc gives an overview of Utah's long and ongoing association with Hollywood.

History of Kane County by Adonis Findlay Robinson contains a history of life in Kane County organized by decade.

In Search of the Old Ones by David Roberts is a somewhat dated but still very readable history of the rediscovery and early preservation by Anglo Americans of Ancestral Puebloan sites in the Four Corners region of the Southwest.

ALSO BY E.B. WHEELER

British Fiction:

Born to Treason

The Royalist's Daughter

The Haunting of Springett Hall

Wishwood (Westwood Gothic)

Moon Hollow (Westwood Gothic)

A Proper Dragon (Dragons of Mayfair 1)

An Elusive Dragon (Dragons of Mayfair 2)

A Subtle Dragon (Dragons of Mayfair 3)

Cruel Magic (Iron & Thorns 1)

Utah Fiction:

No Peace with the Dawn (with Jeffery Bateman)

Letters from the Homefront (Utah at War)

Balm for the Heart (Utah at War)

Bootleggers and Basil (in *The Pathways to the Heart*)

Blood in a Dry Town (Tenny Mateo Mystery 1)

The Bone Map

Nonfiction:

Utah Women: Pioneers, Poets & Politicians

Mysteries of the Old West

ACKNOWLEDGMENTS

I'm grateful to everyone who helped bring this book into being. Thank you to my critique group, The Writers' Cache, for their input and encouragement and to my beta readers Dan, Karen, Keri, and Laura for their invaluable feedback. And as always, my gratitude goes to my husband and children; I couldn't do this without their support.

ABOUT THE AUTHOR

E.B. Wheeler is the author of over a dozen books of history, historical fiction, and historical fantasy, including Whitney Award finalists *Born to Treason, A Proper Dragon,* and *Cruel Magic,* as well as several short stories, magazine articles, and scripts for educational software programs. She has a B.A. in history with an English minor from BYU and graduate degrees in history and landscape architecture from Utah State University. In addition to writing, she sometimes consults about historic preservation and teaches history, and she loves gardening, folk music, reading, and traveling with her husband and kids.

Find more about her books at ebwheeler.com

www.ingramcontent.com/pod-product-compliance
Lightning Source LLC
Chambersburg PA
CBHW051242170626
46809CB00004B/1451